LEARNING TO LOVE AGAIN

LEARNING TO LOVE AGAIN

Chrissie Loveday

CHIVERS

British Library Cataloguing in Publication Data available

This Large Print edition published by BBC Audiobooks Ltd, Bath, 2010
Published by arrangement with the author

U.K. Hardcover ISBN 978 1 408 45794 8
U.K. Softcover ISBN 978 1 408 45795 5

Printed and bound in Great Britain by
CPI Antony Rowe, Chippenham and Eastbourne

ANNA MAKES A FRIEND

'Please Holly, be a good girl. Mummy really does have to go to work now. Aunt Lucy will look after you and you'll have lots of fun.'

'No,' shouted the two, almost three-year-old, stamping her little foot. Anna closed her eyes briefly. Her daughter had quickly learned the power of the word *no* and used it as often as she could.

'Now you're being silly. Please Holly, do as I ask. Look, there's Jackie in the garden. I'm sure he'd love you to throw a ball for him.' She pushed open the door and the toddler ran out, picking up the dog's ball and throwing it wildly into the air, still shouting, 'No!' The little Jack Russell, owned by the family next door, ran over and leapt to catch the ball, missing it and falling over. Holly shrieked with pleasure and continued to run around shouting, 'No!' Aunt Lucy stood behind Anna, watching and laughing at the pair.

'Don't worry, love. She'll be fine. You get yourself off to work. She can let off a bit of steam outside and then I'll get her breakfast ready. Good job next door's dog likes coming into our garden to play.'

'Thank you. You really are a treasure. What would I have done without you?' She gave her aunt a quick hug.

1

'Go on with you. It's my pleasure. I'm glad to have the place alive again. Since your uncle went, I've rattled round like a pea on a drum. We help each other.'

Anna got into her little blue car and set out for the Health Centre. It wasn't far from Lucy's home, but her work as Community Midwife took her all over the local area.

It was a glorious morning and she looked forward to driving round the quiet lanes of Cornwall. It was a different matter in the height of summer when everywhere was filled with visitors. Emmets as they were known locally. But they brought life to the county and much needed income.

Now, in early spring, everywhere was a pure delight. There were wild flowers tucked into every little nook and cranny, patches of colour to brighten the darkest of stone walls.

'I'm so lucky to have a home here,' she whispered. So lucky that Lucy was able to take us in. Had it not been for her aunt, she would have been quite desperate. After Ben had died, she was left with scarcely anything. He had never even known she was pregnant. Would he have gone off in his boat, had he known about the baby? Would she ever forget that dreadful evening?

She swallowed hard and parked in her usual place outside the modern building that was the Health Centre for the large village of St Pirian and several other villages, too small to have

2

their own facilities. She sighed. It was time to forget the past and move forward, however impossible it seemed at times.

'Morning, Anna,' called Maggie from the reception desk. 'Your list's in your pigeon hole.'

'Thanks, Maggie. Efficient as ever.' She picked up the typed sheet and went into her office. She loved the set-up here. She was able to form a really good relationship with the patients. Nothing could ever compare with the joy of a safe delivery of a new life. She glanced down the list of calls she's been asked to make and nodded to herself. She expected one or two of her patients to need extra reassurance and quickly planned her route. There was a noise from Reception and she raised her head to listen, then went out into the corridor to see if she was able to help.

'I'm sorry, madam, but you can't see a doctor immediately. There's a queue waiting and all the doctors are busy.'

'But my little boy's been sick. He needs to see a doctor right away.' The woman was angry, belligerent and quite unwilling to listen to anything that was being said to her.

'If you'll just take a seat, I'll see if I can fit you in as soon as one of the doctors is free.' Maggie sounded quite exasperated.

'It's just not good enough. I have a sick child here . . .'

'What's the problem?' Doctor Meredith

asked, coming from his consulting room. He was about to leave for his rounds. Maggie quickly explained and he took the woman and her child into his room. The other patients in the waiting room looked slightly cross.

'Seems you only have to make a noise and you can jump the queue,' said one of the older ladies, very loudly. Maggie shook her head and then gave a shrug towards Anna.

'You have a system and everyone thinks they should be able to get round it. Joe's too kind for his own good.'

'At least he's quietened things down in here,' Anna said wryly. 'Doctor Meredith hasn't been here long enough to know the devious nature of some of our patients. Well, I'd better be on my way. I should be back early this afternoon.'

She picked up her medical bag and the files of patient records. There seemed to be so much more paper these days. There had been enough when she trained and first began her work but it was so much worse now. Computers were supposed to have made it easier, she grumbled, but it seemed everything still came in multiple copies on sheets of paper.

It was a busy morning and the time flew by. Soon it was almost lunchtime as she was driving along her beloved quiet lanes. She arrived at one of the tiny hamlets, where a row of six houses nestled in a valley leading down to a cove, so well concealed that only the locals knew of its existence. Once she had visited her last patient of the morning, she planned to take her sandwiches and sit next to the sea and enjoy a brief break.

'You're looking good,' she told her patient, Sarah. 'Not long now. I'm pleased you've been doing the exercises. Are you managing to rest a bit more during the day?'

'Not too bad. But you know how it is, what with Damian away most of the time and the toddler to manage. Mrs Brierley's been taking Jamie for an hour or two when she can. But poor soul, she's got her husband to look after. He's not been well either.' Sarah's own husband worked on the fishing boats and was often out at sea for several days at a time.

'You cope wonderfully, Sarah. I just hope Damian will be home in time for the birth. Let's just check your blood pressure.' She wrapped the cuff around her patient's arm and inflated it. She listened as the beat stabilised and as Sarah tensed, she spoke again to calm her. 'That's great. You're doing really well. Everything in place. Actually, you are quite advanced considering the birth date.' She looked at her records and frowned. It couldn't be another month away but she didn't want to alarm Sarah. 'You know, we ought to consider booking you into the Maternity Unit in case Damian's not back. I don't like you staying here on your own in this remote spot.'

'I'll be fine. Damian's taking time off once we're closer to the time. I've got my final scan next week, so that should tell us something.'

'OK. Well, call the surgery if you've any problems. I'm going to sneak down your lane now and have my lunch. OK if I leave my car outside for a bit?'

'Sure. Thanks, Anna. Hope you enjoy your lunch.'

Anna locked her things in the boot and collected her sandwiches. She noticed another car in the lane and saw Joe Meredith emerging from the neighbouring cottage. Her heart gave a small leap of pleasure as she saw him. How silly, she thought.

'Hello. What are you doing here?' he asked, crossing to her and giving her the sort of smile that did strange things to her insides.

'Just about to eat my lunch down on the beach. One of my mums lives here.' She nodded towards the house.

'I've been visiting Mr Brierley. He's not well, poor man. His angina's always a problem, but I'm a bit concerned about him today. Sorry. Shop talk, but as you know the family . . . Look, I know it's an awful cheek, but do you mind if I join you? I've just bought a pack of sandwiches from the shop back there and if I don't eat something soon, I'll probably pass out completely.'

'Feel free.' Anna smiled. She certainly had no objection to sharing her time with a new

6

colleague. Especially one who was young and good looking . . . not that she was interested in men at all, not since Ben. It was just nice to have some male company for a change. They walked companionably down the steep slope to the sparkling sea.

'Wow. This is pretty special isn't it?' Joe ran forward excitedly, like a small boy. Anna smiled at his enthusiasm. 'Come on, let's paddle.' He undid his garish tic, covered in cartoon characters. He dragged his shoes and socks off and dipped his toe in the icy water, yelling as he did so.

'Not as warm as it looks?' she called out laughing. 'You won't get me in there for a pension.'

'Coward. It's great once you're in. Come on or I'll be forced to drag you down here.'

She sat herself firmly on a rock and watched him. No wonder all the female staff were talking about him and the patients asking for him. He was probably everyone's fantasy of the perfect, dreamy doctor. She gave a small sigh and turned her attention to her lunch. She lifted the lid of her box.

As usual, Lucy had put in a lot more than just a sandwich. Fruit, a little pack of salad and a couple of tiny sausage rolls. She felt thoroughly spoilt. Joe ran back up the beach and plonked down beside her. He even smelled good . . . something that sprang from fresh air and a light, spicy aftershave.

7

'Your trousers are all wet at the bottom,' she pointed out, dragging her mind back to reality. 'Not quite the way for a respectable doctor to behave.' His smart work suit was looking decidedly worse for wear.

'Who said anything about being respectable? You look most disapproving. Sorry. But I am only a locum. I don't come with the same standard of behaviour as one of the old men of the practice.'

'Why are you still a locum? Why haven't you taken something more permanent?'

His handsome face crinkled as he considered. His eyes were almost the same greenish brown that Ben's were, she noticed with a sudden shiver. The same colour as Holly's. Joe's brown hair was slightly darker than Ben's but it was tipped with blond, as if he spent a lot of time out in the open. He was slightly taller than Ben and though slim, looked muscular and very fit.

'Why am I still a locum? I guess I haven't yet found anywhere I want to settle. Besides, I do have other commitments. Being a locum means I can be a bit more flexible.'

She wondered about his commitments. A wife maybe? She rather hoped not. They chatted easily and half-an-hour whizzed by incredibly fast. He was a most likeable man and she felt totally at ease in his company. She tried to discover more about him, but he was remarkably skilled at avoiding questions with a joke or flippant remark. Instead, she found herself telling him about Holly and the difficulties she found working and tearing herself away from her small child each day.

'Must be tough,' Joe said sympathetically. 'What about your husband? Does he work too?'

'I'm a . . . my husband's dead.'

'Oh, I'm so sorry. But he must have been very young.'

'He was. Only thirty.' Joe reached over and put a very warm, strong hand over hers.

'I'm sorry. I wasn't thinking. Please don't be upset . . . but maybe talking about it might help?'

His eyes were full of concern and she sniffed.

'He drowned. Went out sailing in his boat and never came back. Getting on for three years ago now. I still can't believe it sometimes.' He stared at her and hesitated before asking, 'Was that here? In Cornwall?'

'We used to live nearer Padstow.' He said nothing and looked slightly uncomfortable.

'I suppose I should be getting back. Thanks for your company and I'm sorry if I opened up old wounds.' He stood up and dusted off his trousers. 'You're right, you know. I should try to be more respectable. But then, I wouldn't have the cheek to invite myself to share lunch with a beautiful midwife.'

Much to her amazement, he leaned down

9

and put a finger beneath her chin and lifted her face, staring into her clear blue eyes. 'Come on.' He took her hand and hauled her up to her feet. She was quite speechless.

'Doctor Meredith . . . Joe . . . you must understand, I'm not interested in you . . . in anyone. I have a small daughter and a busy life. Of course I'm flattered. You're a very attractive man and . . .'

'Hey there. Steady on. I'm not proposing to you! Now, we'd better get back, don't you think? Or someone will be talking about us.'

Despite herself, Anna was biting back a smile. It really was rather flattering that a handsome, younger man found her attractive, however wrong she knew it must be. How could she even look at another man when her own beloved husband had died less than three long, lonely years ago?

She sighed. Maybe one day, she should consider letting herself out of this self-imposed emotional isolation, if only for Holly's sake. She needed a man in her life. A father figure. But not now. Not yet. And she certainly would never be looking at someone as temporary as a locum, like Doctor Meredith. He would disappear as quickly as he'd appeared, once Doctor Christopher returned from his course.

She hoped, under the circumstances, that his other commitments didn't include a wife.

'Forget all about this, please,' she demanded.

10

'Race you up the hill,' was his response. 'Come on, let your hair down a bit.' He shot off at a pace she could never match . . . not ever, even when she was younger. She walked sedately up the hill and smiled as she saw he was leaning on his car, panting fit to burst. 'Not as fit as I should be. Must need to work out a bit. You ever go to the gym? You should. It's good for you.'

'You try fitting in a working day and looking after an energetic two-year-old. And covering nights at least twice a week. No time for gyms and the like.'

'You could come with me,' he suggested. 'As my guest. I'm a member of a very exclusive place near Truro.'

'You're too pushy by half,' she told him as she got back into her car. Despite herself, she leaned out of the window and said, 'Thanks for your company. I enjoyed the change but I don't make a habit of this. And please, don't mention it ever again. We do have to work together.'

As she drove away, he made an exaggerated deep bow, his head almost touching his knees as he did so. He gave her a final cheeky wave, which she saw through her rear view mirror. If he didn't amuse her, she might have been very irritated at his presumption. He was obviously rather immature, she tried to tell herself but wasn't convinced. All the same, he was clearly good-hearted and the patients were already asking for him, when they booked appointments.

Perhaps the surgery needed someone who could joke a little and lighten the often rather intense and even gloomy monthly meetings. Her heart was already feeling lighter and his mood had rubbed off on her own.

After she had made one more call to check on the first-time mother to be, one who was suffering from a major case of nerves, she went back to the Health Centre to run her ante-natal class. She judged there was just time to complete her notes on the morning visits, and set to work. There was a tap on the door and before she could call out, the door opened and a hand appeared, holding out a red rose. The hand reached for the shelf inside the door and deposited the rose on the top.

The door closed again and she was left staring. She opened the door and looked out at the empty corridor. It had to be Joe. No one else would ever do anything so romantic, so foolish. She picked up the delicate bloom and sniffed the fragrance. She filled a small jug with water and stood the rose on her desk, wondering whose garden was now short of one red rose.

ANOTHER CHANCE FOR LOVE?

'How's my favourite girl?' called Anna as she put her key in the lock. She heard a pattering of bare feet running across the wooden floor of the hall.

'Mummy, Mummy. Went to the park. Fell down.' Anna was swamped by a wet and grubby hug as her little girl flung herself at her mother.

'Hello, darling,' called Lucy from the kitchen. 'The kettle's on. Won't be a minute. Good day?'

They sat on the kitchen chairs, one at each side of the table, grown up accounts of their days interspersed with Holly's excited chatter. Anna couldn't help being slightly jealous of the things they did together, her aunt and small daughter. If things had been different, she would have been the one visiting the park and sticking plasters on grazed knees. She adored her work and had always intended that she would return to midwifery once her family had grown up a little. But it was never meant to be this way, someone else caring for the little girl while she was at work.

'I've made a casserole for supper, so you can relax and play with Holly for an hour or so. I'm going to have a little rest, if you don't mind. That cold last month really took it out of me

13

and I feel shattered.'

'Are you sure there's nothing else wrong?' Anna asked anxiously. Her aunt had never had children of her own and for someone over fifty to begin caring for a lively toddler for the first time in her life, was rather more tiring than she may have expected. Lucy reassured her niece and went for her rest.

Mother and daughter played together for a while and then Anna scrambled an egg for Holly's supper. They settled down to look at some books and all too soon, it was time for the little girl's bath and bedtime. They were precious moments and Anna gave herself to Holly unstintingly. She had to be a mother and father to the child and though Lucy was wonderful to them both, there were her own needs to be considered. Her hobbies had been generously pushed to one side when they came to live with her and Anna felt guilty that her aunt rarely had time for her painting now.

Until Holly went to school, she could see no alternative to the situation. She tucked the little girl into her little bed and went downstairs. She put the kettle on for a drink when she heard the phone ringing. She rushed down to answer it before Lucy was disturbed.

'Anna?' said an anxious voice. 'It's Sarah. I think the baby's coming. It's very early, I know but I don't know what to do.'

'Have you rung the night service?'

'Well, no, I so wanted you to deliver me, as

14

you know. You did promise . . . but as it's at least a month early . . . oh please, can you come? Ooh.' There was a pause as Sarah obviously had another contraction.

'I think maybe we'd better get you into hospital. You're probably right. The baby's clearly coming early. I did wonder whether your dates were accurate this morning.'

'But what am I going to do about Jamie? I can't leave him. Damian's not back yet.'

'Just hold on. I'll be with you in ten minutes or so.'

Anna went into action. Once she'd checked on Holly, she went to wake Lucy to explain that she had to go out. Lucy was in a deep sleep and she felt a moment's concern about waking her aunt.

'You can stay in bed. Holly's fast asleep already. I'm not sure what's going to happen. We might end up at the hospital, but I'll call and let you know. Are you sure you're OK?'

'I'm fine, love. Just a bit tired. I'll get up in a minute. And I can listen out for Holly if she needs anything. Don't worry. I didn't realise you were on call tonight.'

'I wasn't. Special case,' she called back as she ran downstairs.

*   *   *

She drove slightly faster than was absolutely safe, anxious to reach Sarah and see exactly

15

what was going on. It was her second pregnancy and had seemed like a textbook case. The dates were slightly in question, but all the signs had indicated that she should go to full term, which should have been in four weeks time. But then, many babies seemed to make their own decision about when they were due to appear and this was obviously one of them. She parked outside the little house for the second time that day, grabbed her medical bag and ran up the path.

Sarah opened the door, leaning against the frame and already looking grey and sweaty.

'OK. Lie down on the sofa and let me take a look at you.'

She then swung into action, collecting the birthing pack from the car, the portable gas and air machine, just in case it was needed and the monitoring equipment. She then phoned for an ambulance to stand-by.

Anna got everything ready for when the baby arrived. There wasn't even time to attach the monitor as everything was happening so fast. She made sure there was somewhere ready to put the baby, always watching her patient carefully.

Tears and laughter, relief and anxiety all rushed out in the next few seconds. Anna felt the tears pricking in her own eyes. There was nothing in the world like the feeling of helping a new life into existence. She had the best job ever and no matter how many births she attended, every single one was unique and special. Sarah lay back, waiting for Anna to lie her new daughter on to her chest.

'Let me see her,' demanded the new mother. Anna covered the tiny child in a soft sheet and gently laid her on her mother. Just as everything was over, the ambulance arrived.

'Need any help?' asked the cheery paramedic.

'You're too late! Typical, come when the hard work's over and done with. This one was something of a record.'

'What, no problems?' he asked.

'None at all. Perfect delivery. And the baby seems fine. Looks pretty much full term actually. I'll just weigh her for the records. She's gorgeous, Sarah. Congratulations. You both still need to get checked over, though.'

'Oh Anna, I don't know how to thank you. You were marvellous. She's been brilliant,' she told the ambulance men.

'Course she is. We only employ marvellous people. Now, I think we'd getter get you and this young lady off to hospital to check you over.'

'But I've got a little boy asleep upstairs. I can't leave him.'

'Don't worry. I'll sort something out,' Anna reassured her. 'You'll probably be home tomorrow, if everything's normal. It certainly looks as if it will be. Can I get in touch with Damian?'

17

'I've got his mobile number. On the side table by the phone. If he's in range, you'll get him on that. I didn't think to call him before. If you can't get him on the mobile, you'll have to call the office. They might be able to contact him on the radio. The number's are all on the pad.'

'Leave it with me. I'll see what I can do.'

*   *   *

Once the ambulance had left, Anna cleared everything away. She looked in on the sleeping child and left him undisturbed. Next she tried to contact the father. She felt a great sense of relief when he answered his mobile and an even greater one when he said his boat was already in port and in the circumstances, he could leave the boat before they'd cleared the catch.

Anna suddenly felt totally exhausted. It was almost ten o'clock and she had eaten nothing since lunch. She actually felt rather faint, she realised. She phoned home to see if all was well and went to check on Jamie. Reassured, she ran quickly to next door to see if Mrs Brierley could help out. To her surprise, Dr Meredith, Joe, was there, repacking his medical bag.

'Hello, again,' he said, looking pleased to see her. 'I'm afraid Mr Brierley's taken a turn for the worse. His wife called me out and

I've given him something to relieve his pain.' Mrs Brierley came back into the room. 'I think we'd better arrange to get him to hospital in the morning to check things over. He may eventually need an operation to sort him out.' Anna felt he was speaking to her as a fellow professional and smiled reassuringly at Mrs Brierley.

'Just considering possibilities. We'll organise a scan. No need to be alarmed. He should sleep through now, so we'll leave him in peace for tonight. We'll get him into hospital as soon as we can tomorrow. So, Anna, what are you doing here?'

'Sarah's just delivered a daughter. All very unexpected and very quick. I came to see if Mrs Brierley could look after Jamie for a while but obviously not. Don't worry. I'll stay till Damian gets here. He shouldn't be long. Sorry to disturb you.'

Mrs Brierley was delighted to hear the news and most apologetic about not being available at such an important time. Anna let herself out and went back into the silent house next door. She made some coffee and sat down on the sofa. The door opened and Dr Meredith came in.

'Hi. Thought I'd keep you company till the happy father arrives. Mind if I make some coffee for myself?'

'Well, I'm sure Sarah wouldn't mind. But really, I'll be fine. You don't need to stay. I doubt it will be long before Damian gets here. Oh, thank you for the rose by the way.'

'My pleasure. I'd like to if that's all right with you. Give us a bit of time to talk. I'm afraid I might have made rather an idiot of myself today. Can we start over? Pretend anything that upset you, didn't happen?'

'I suppose so. Not sure what you mean though. You weren't to know about my husband's accident.' She couldn't help but be pleased he was here with her. He smiled his special smile which had the strange effect on her as before.

'I want to know all about you,' he said as he sat beside her. 'So, tell me why you're living with your aunt? No parents to help out?'

'My parents were killed in an air crash soon after Ben and I were married.'

'I'm sorry. That must have been tough for you. Gosh you've really been through it, haven't you?' He put out a comforting hand and held her own for a while. 'Didn't you have a home of your own, somewhere with Ben?'

'Well, yes. Not that it's any of your business.' She pulled her hand away, as if she were trying to break contact with his seemingly endless questions. It was much nicer when he'd been holding it, she realised.

'I know it isn't, but I want to know what makes you tick. What lies behind those beautiful but rather sad eyes of yours?' He looked at her, his head slightly tilted on one side. She had to smile at his expression.

'We had a home. One with a very large mortgage. Ben also wanted to start his own business so we were even deeper in debt.'

'Didn't you carry insurance? Life policy or something?'

'You ever tried to claim when there's no body? No death certificate? I had to wait for goodness knows how long till it was certain Ben wasn't coming back. We had to apply for an inquest. All very complicated and most unpleasant. In the meantime, I discovered that Ben had stopped paying the insurance premiums anyway. He'd cleared out the bank account, presumably when he was launching the business. It left me with a house whose value was less than the money we owed and payments I couldn't possibly afford. It was a horrible mess altogether. All that to cope with as well as losing Ben and being pregnant.'

'I see. You poor soul.' He looked admiringly at her. She was so lovely, he thought. He wanted to hold her. To protect her from the terrible hurt she had suffered. He dragged himself back to the conversation, trying not to let slip that he knew a whole lot more than she suspected. 'But you managed to come through it remarkably well. There was a thorough search for him. They didn't find the boat or anything else. No trace at all.' He wasn't asking, she could see. It was as if he already knew. It had been in all the local papers and on the television and radio news so obviously he'd heard about it. Put two and two together and realised it was her.

'You've clearly heard the story. It's been very hard to find closure. I had to sell the house and by the time I moved out, I was almost due to give birth. I was fortunate my Aunt Lucy could help out. Her own husband had died some years earlier and she had a largish house, plenty of room for me and the baby. Once I'd recovered, I had to return to work and she now looks after Holly each day.'

'And Ben knew nothing of the baby?'

'He didn't know I was pregnant. I was going to tell him that very night.' Her expression changed to one of sadness as the memories flooded back. 'He got later and later and I got crosser and crosser, thinking he'd gone to the pub or something. Eventually, I phoned the sailing club and discovered he'd never returned. He'd filed his plan as usual, saying where he was going.

'They began a search the next morning.' She stared down at her fingers, working to control her emotions. 'I'm sorry. I shouldn't have burdened you with my troubles. I don't know what came over me. I never talk about it to anyone. I'm sorry.'

'Stop saying you're sorry. I'm flattered that you felt able to talk to me. I'm . . .'

The door rattled and Damian burst in.

'Oh, Anna. Sorry. I didn't realise you had

22

someone with you.'

'This is Doctor Meredith. He was visiting your neighbour and thought he'd come to keep me company for a while. Till you got back.'

'Hi, Doc. How is everything? Can't wait to see them. I suppose I can't go now, can I? What about Jamie?'

'He hasn't stirred. Slept through the lot. He still has no idea he has a sister. Sarah and the baby are at the hospital, hopefully sound asleep themselves by now. If everything's OK, they should discharge her tomorrow. But you can go in to see her first thing, in any case. You may even be able to bring her home with you.'

'Gosh. I can't believe it. All this was going on while I sat on the boat. We were just beginning to unload the catch when you called. I'd planned to be with her. To see this one born. You just never know, do you?'

'Babies are always a law unto themselves. Congratulations, Damian. We'll be off then,' Anna said wearily. 'I'll see you soon. I'll call round tomorrow sometime, once we know what's happening.'

The doctor and the midwife went out to their cars.

'I didn't realise you were on-call this evening.'

'I wasn't,' she replied. 'But I'd promised Sarah I'd try to be the one to deliver the baby. Come to that, I didn't know you did night calls, either.'

'I don't. But Mrs Brierley seemed so upset, I gave her my mobile number in case she needed anything out of hours.'

'So you're an old softy at heart, as bad as me. Doesn't go with the madcap image you try to present.'

'I do no such thing. Too late to argue now. You must be worn out. Get yourself home and go to bed. Unless maybe there's something else you'd rather do? No? Thought not.' He pulled a sad face.

'I actually don't know if I'd rather just fall asleep or have a huge meal. I'm starving. We were just about to have supper when the phone rang.'

'I could feed you something. There's bound to be a chip shop open or somewhere doing late night food.'

'I expect Lucy will have kept me something. I'd better get back. See you tomorrow. And thanks.'

'For what?'

'Thanks for listening. I hope you realise, I didn't even cry this time . . . when I talked about Ben's accident. That may be a first in itself.'

He touched her arm again and for a moment, life itself seemed to be suspended for a brief moment. There was definitely something between them . . . some chemistry she could not explain. Almost breathless, she got into her car and gave him what she hoped looked like a casual wave, as she drove away. Perhaps she was simply getting used to the fact that her husband had disappeared without a trace. She should be after all this time. But huge pangs of guilt washed over her. She shouldn't be getting over him. She owed it to Holly to keep her father alive in her own memory as well as the child's.

She couldn't see the look on her colleague's face as she drove away. The usually sunny expression had quite left his features and he looked troubled. He was fighting with his own dilemma. What was it about her that made his heart lurch? He knew he had to tell her something, but it could ruin his chances of seeing her eyes lose their haunted look. Something that could finish their relationship even before it began.

EMOTIONS ARE STIRRED

Despite her late night, Anna was awake early enough to give Holly her breakfast the next morning.

'Did you get anything to eat when you finally got in?' Lucy asked anxiously.

'I was too exhausted. I'd got over feeling hungry by the time I got back.'

'And everything was OK? No dramas?'

'It was amazing. So quick.'

'You do love your work, don't you?' Lucy smiled at the enthusiasm.

'Of course I do. But sometimes, I'd like there to be a bit more time around me. I've got to write up the report this morning, between a hundred and one other things.'

'You need to take it easy too. Have some time for you. Do something just for yourself.'

'Oh and listen who's talking? You haven't picked up a paintbrush in months. In fact, I feel very guilty about it. I'll take Holly away one weekend soon and you can have a complete rest from us both. We can go to see Ben's parents. They should see their granddaughter occasionally.'

'Really, there's no need. But, yes, maybe you're right. You should let them see their granddaughter. It will be upsetting for you, though. You know it will.'

'I have to do it though, Lucy. I don't know why but they seem to hold me responsible for Ben's death. They seem to think I should have alerted the rescue services much earlier. But how could I? Ben would have been furious if there was nothing wrong and I'd called out the lifeboat. All the same, I do wonder if I'd acted sooner . . .'

'Now, Anna. That's enough. I'm going to cook you some bacon and eggs and you will sit down and eat it properly. No rushing off. After working all of last night on your own, you can surely be allowed a little break?'

'Actually, I wasn't alone.' Lucy raised her eyebrows. 'The new locum, Joe Meredith, happened to be next door and he kept me company till the father arrived.'

'Nice. I'll get on with breakfast.' Wisely, she said no more, but didn't miss the slight flush in Anna's cheeks and wasn't that an extra sparkle in her eyes today?

Anna sat sipping her coffee, while Lucy fussed round her, cooking an enormous breakfast. She realised how hungry she really was and tucked in with great relish. She ate a couple of rounds of toast afterwards and leaned back in her chair.

'Thanks Lucy,' Anna said gratefully. 'I don't know what we'd do without you.'

'Hush with you. Now get yourself off to work. And make sure you get an evening off to make up for last night. Go to the pictures or something.'

'I'd hate to go to the cinema on my own. But thanks for the thought.'

'Maybe you could go with someone from work. The new locum maybe? It's time you started thinking about your own future. You can't grieve forever. Ben would have hated that.'

*   *   *

She drove to work, thinking about her life. Would she never be free of the memory of those days when Ben disappeared? She'd spent hours watching and waiting for news. Everyone was certain he'd gone down with his boat but there had never been any trace of either. No body had ever been recovered and not so much as a lifebelt or piece of debris had been found.

She had asked everyone she could think of, how it could have happened to such an experienced sailor? Most of all, she wanted to know why nothing had been found, but it couldn't be explained. Currents, tides, winds that were blowing at the time had all been checked and evaluated for a possible site but there was nothing. For months, she had expected to get a call from some distant place to say he was alive and had lost his memory but no such luck. With a sigh, she drove into her parking space and tried to move her mind on to thoughts of her day ahead.

* * *

'How are you today?' Joe asked. He looked as weary as she felt.

'Tired, but fine. Once the adrenaline flow stopped, I seemed to collapse, but one of Lucy's ginormous breakfasts has put me right. How's Mr Brierley?'

'OK. I've arranged for him to go in to Landris for a check-up and hopefully it will give Mrs B a bit of respite. I enjoyed talking last night. I wondered . . . I know what you said about everything, but I wondered if you'd have dinner with me one evening?'

'It's very kind of you, but as I explained, I do need to spend every possible moment with Holly. I don't ever go out in the evenings.'

'Surely she goes to bed quite early? She's only young. And you were out last night.'

'I was working,' she snapped rather too quickly. 'No. It isn't a good idea. I don't want you to think we . . . well, we might . . . No. It's just not possible. Not practical. Besides, I'm older than you are.'

'Almost ready to draw a pension, I'd say. For heaven's sake. I'm only asking you to have dinner with me. Not commit for life.'

'Please keep your voice down. People can hear.'

'So what?' he said only marginally more

quietly. He glared at her and turned away, storming off to his office. 'Suit yourself,' she heard him mutter. She bit her lip wishing she'd handled it better. There was nothing she'd have liked more than to have dinner with him, she realised.

'So, the gorgeous Doctor Meredith has chosen you to lavish his attention, has he?' Maggie said with a huge grin on her face.

'We simply worked together yesterday. He was . . . saying thank you, I suppose,' she blustered.

'He can say thank you to me any time he likes.' She caught Anna's glare. 'Oh no. Don't tell me you knocked him back? You didn't . . . couldn't refuse him?'

'For heaven's sake, stop gossiping, Maggie. I'm not going out with him or anyone else. I have responsibilities; you know I do. My husband's . . .'

'Oh, Anna,' she chided. 'Isn't it about time you came out of your cave? You're an attractive young woman. You should get out and do things, not just work yourself into the ground. I know you've had it tough but you're too dedicated by half. Look at last night. I bet you don't take time off in lieu.'

'How did you know about last night? I haven't written up my report yet.'

'Doctor Meredith told me. Mind you, he's pretty dedicated himself, for a locum, don't you think? He was working out of hours with

Mr Brierley. You're obviously two of a kind. Though I don't see you dashing off to the lifeboat in your spare time.'

'Lifeboat? I don't know what you're talking about.'

'He's a R.N.L.I. volunteer. Mans the lifeboat whenever he's needed. I thought you knew.'

'I hardly know him at all,' she said thoughtfully. 'Must get on. I'll see you later. Oh, have you got my list of calls for today?' She picked up the sheet and glanced down it. There was nothing urgent and she saw she could fit everything in with her routine rounds. Lifeboat man, eh? That must have been what he meant about other commitments.

She couldn't cope with someone else who went out to sea. Not after Ben. Apart from looking at waves from the safety of the beach, she wanted nothing more to do with the ocean.

*　　　*　　　*

When Anna called the hospital, she heard that Sarah had already been collected by Damian and their little boy.

'They were both fine. You did a good job there.' The sister at the small Maternity Unit had become a good friend over the months and they worked well together when it was necessary. 'We must get together soon,' Joanna suggested. 'Go for a drink or something.'

'That would be nice. We'll fix a date, soon. Bye.'

'Oh, so you do have time for occasional dates then,' said a voice from the open door. Joe was leaning against the frame and staring at her. He had the same smile on his face that had affected her so much yesterday.

'That was private, Joe. I've told you; I can't go out with you, not now, not ever. I'm not ready for any sort of relationship, casual or otherwise.'

'I thought we would go down to Porthcullion tomorrow evening, around eight o'clock. We could have a bite to eat at the pub and then there's a band on afterwards. I can collect you from home and I'll even let you introduce me to your Aunt. Lucy wasn't it? So she can see you are in respectable company.'

'Joe, please stop hassling me. I can't go out with you. Really. It isn't right.'

'Why not? My one bad habit, I should warn you of. I'm very persistent and never take no for an answer.'

'Oh, Joe.' Despite herself, Anna found she was smiling. 'Why me? I've told you I'm not available and that I don't want . . .'

'Any sort of relationship. Does that include a relationship with a wonderful dish of steamed local sole, garnished with lemon butter and fresh prawns, with new potatoes and salad? Even if you hate the company, that fish is to die for.'

She felt herself smiling and in a moment of weakness, gave in. She realised just how much she wanted to spend time with him, despite all her doubts.

'OK. Why not? But this is just for dinner. A one off. Just to shut you up.'

'Excellent. I'll be round about seven tomorrow.'

'You said eight.'

'That was before you told me I had to meet your aunt. Must give her time to get to love me as much as you do.'

'For heavens sake. Be serious for five minutes. Why me?'

'Because you need to be loved. I want to see the sadness leave your eyes for a while. I want to see your smile and most of all; I want to get to know you. I quite fancy you too.' She found herself blushing at his words.

He breezed out. Anna smiled as she pulled out the report forms to complete for her delivery last night. However much she pretended, Joe was certainly a breath of fresh air after the miserable faces she seemed to see much of the time. The rest of the doctors in the practice were all rather elderly and resistant to all forms of change. The senior partner was mainly concerned in keeping his budget under tight rein. Acupuncture . . . that could be an interesting addition to the treatment offered by the Health Centre. She wondered what Doctor Whittaker would make of that idea.

*   *   *

Lucy was absolutely delighted that her niece was going out the following evening and made a great deal of being pleased that Anna was taking her advice.

'So who is he?' she asked. 'Why haven't you mentioned him before?'

She passed on the little she knew about Joe Meredith, doing her best to make it clear he was just a colleague and that they were going out socially primarily to discuss what he knew about alternative therapies. In fact, she was so convincing that she almost began to believe it herself. It somehow made her feel better about the whole thing. Less guilty to Ben's memory.

By the time the following evening arrived, Anna was in a state of nerves she had difficulty hiding. She had put Holly to bed rather earlier than usual, not wanting her to meet a stranger at this stage. She took a quick shower and brushed her short dark hair into its usual crown of curls. She ransacked her wardrobe to find the right clothes to wear.

She didn't want to look as if she had dressed up but neither did she want to look scruffy, as if she didn't care. In fact, she realised it was so long since she had been out anywhere at all, she no longer knew what people wore to go out! She finally chose some rather ordinary cream trousers and a blue silky shirt to make the outfit look slightly dressier.

'Hope I'll do,' she said to Lucy.

'You look fine love. I suspect he's a bit more special than you're letting on.'

'Of course not. It's just that, well, he's a bit younger than me and I don't want him to think he's out with an old frump.'

'You'll never be a frump. Now, should I offer him a drink, do you think?'

'I shouldn't think so. He's driving. Oh, there he is now. You're sure I look all right?' Lucy laughed and nodded. 'I'll go and let him in. I assume you want to meet him.'

'I'll let him in myself,' Lucy insisted. 'You just practice relaxing for a moment. Breathe deeply. You're all of a dither.'

'No I'm not. Course I'm not.' But really she was, she had to admit.

She heard them laughing within seconds. Lucy pushed open the door and ushered him into the pretty sitting room. He was wearing a pair of cream chinos and a chocolate-coloured shirt which suited him perfectly.

'Here she is. All ready. Now, can I get you anything? Coffee, tea. Or something stronger?'

'That's kind, but I'm driving. Thank you. I'll allow myself a single glass of something with the meal. It's really nice to meet you. I've heard a lot about you.'

Anna was amused to see Lucy falling instantly under his spell. Joe certainly could be most charming and he even seemed to realise that his usual sense of fun needed to be curbed just a little for her aunt. After half an hour, he suggested they should leave. Lucy showed them out, muttering, 'He's gorgeous,' in her ear as she went out. She turned and gave her a hug.

'Don't you get any ideas,' she muttered under her breath.

*　　　*　　　*

'So, Doctor Meredith, are you going to tell me something about yourself?' she asked, once they were sitting in front of plates of delicious looking food.

'Not a lot to tell. I trained and qualified. Had several locum jobs but never seemed to find anywhere I really wanted to make my home. I can't bear to leave Cornwall, if the truth were told. Think I've got roots digging deep into the granite and they won't be parted for long.'

'Do your parents live here?'

'Like you, I don't have any parents. They died just as I got my place in med school. My sister and I became very close after they died. She's a couple of years older than me. She also lives in Cornwall, not far from here. Happily married with two kids. Boys, and a real handful they are too.'

She felt sympathy for Joe. He too had suffered loss and must have struggled to get his training. It was remarkable that he seemed so cheerful all the time. Perhaps it was his own way of coping with what must have been a devastating loss at the time.

'It must have been difficult.'

'One moves on. You'd like my sister, Evie. She's great and I'm looking forward to introducing you both. Now, what do you think of this fish? Pretty good isn't it?'

'Wonderful. You were right. I could have a serious relationship with this. I don't think it will be a very long-lasting one though,' she said, trying to lighten the mood.

'You should smile more often. It suits you. You're very lovely you know. I feel quite jealous of all the years you've lived without my knowing you.'

'Be serious. You're too full of jokes. I don't know whether to believe you or not half the time.'

'OK. I think I want to be very serious about you. I know, in fact.' He held his hand up as she was about to speak. 'I know, we've only just met. It's very early days, but I have never felt this attracted to a woman for a very long time. Besides, you have all the right qualities.'

'I do?' she asked blushing.

'You live in Cornwall. That has to mean something.'

She laughed, relieved to be back on a less intense level. One that she could cope with. A more serious expression flitted across his handsome face.

'Actually, there is something you should know about me.' Anna stared, wondering what revelation was coming next. 'I'm a crew member of the R.N.L.I. Lifeboats? I'm a volunteer and go out on rescue missions when I'm needed.'

She nodded her head. 'I'd heard. And yes, it is a bit of a problem. I couldn't cope with another man who regularly goes out to sea and puts himself in danger.'

He pressed his lips together and frowned. 'I had a feeling you'd say that. I suppose I could give it up but it's part of my family tradition. My dad. My uncle. Various cousins. They've all taken their turn. But that's not everything I needed to say. I was actually part of the team who went in search of your Ben. That's why I knew the story so well. Nobody ever wanted to call off the search, but there comes a time when you know it's pointless. I'm sorry, Anna.'

The delicious food stuck in her throat as she tried to come to terms with facing one of Ben's would-be rescuers.

'Tell me something,' she gasped. 'If we'd called you out earlier, would it have made a difference?'

'I doubt it. If his boat was going down, it would have been very quick and there would have been nothing we could do. He had a radio on board so we'd have responded anyway, if he'd hit something. Someone would be sure to have called in.'

'I see. So you think he must have sunk immediately?'

'I guess so. We had no clue of his whereabouts, despite the plan he'd left. We couldn't work out how far he'd gone in the time and we could only follow the leads we had from possible sightings. We broadened the search as widely as was feasible. Not a single trace was ever found.'

'That in itself sounded strange. You'd think something might have been found, if only a bit of debris. Could it be that he meant to disappear? You know, sailed to some other place and began again?'

She could see from the expression in his eyes that Joe sensed the depth of turmoil behind her questions. Questions she'd posed a thousand times, but had never believed.

'I'd have thought it would be impossible for any boat to disappear without trace. There's usually something torn off or fuel leaks that float up. But not in this case. I can see why it's been so difficult for you. You must have spent so many hours just wondering.' He put his hand over hers again and gave it a squeeze. 'Come on. Eat up now. You need to consider what lies ahead in the way of a pudding.' He leaned over and kissed her gently on the cheek. 'Enough sadness and soul searching for one evening. Thanks for being here with me. I appreciate it.'

'Thank you too,' Anna whispered and meant it. Maybe there was something ahead for them both but at the moment, they could simply enjoy each other's company occasionally. Perhaps it could remain casual. Perhaps not.

AN INVITATION FROM JOE

'So, how was it?' Lucy asked the minute Anna returned home. She barely had time to remove her jacket.

'Fine. Lovely. We should go to that pub one lunchtime. It's lovely food.'

'I wasn't asking about the food. Joe, what's he like?'

Her face was serious for a moment but then she burst out laughing. 'He's lovely. Quite mad, well eccentric perhaps, but a very nice man and very good company.'

'Excellent. So when are you seeing him again?'

'Tomorrow. At work.'

'I meant seeing him, seeing him.'

'Take that gleam out of your eyes. He's a friend and that's all he can ever be. As a matter of fact, he's a lifeboat man. He was part of the search team that was looking for Ben.'

Her aunt's jaw dropped and she paled. She grasped Anna's hand and whispered soft comforting words.

'It's OK, Lucy. Really. Only, you do see why I can't ever let myself get fond of him, even if it did move on further. I daren't risk falling for another sailor. It isn't fair to Holly for one thing. If she ever thought there would be a new daddy in her life, it would have to be someone who didn't do anything dangerous. But, hey, we're all getting ahead of ourselves here. I've only been out for a pub meal with the man, after all.'

'You sound to me as though you're trying to convince yourself there's no future with him. But even you have to admit, he's rather dishy.'

Anna smiled and nodded. It was going to be difficult seeing him every day and knowing that she mustn't allow herself to show any encouragement to him. Even thinking of him set her heart beating faster, which was quite ridiculous under the circumstances.

'I must get to bed. I feel totally wiped out. I'll just look in on Holly.'

'She's fine. Never stirred all evening. Sleep well.'

'Thanks. And you.' Anna looked down at her little daughter and touched her soft blonde hair. She was beginning to look more and more like Ben. Whatever she wanted for herself and the future, Holly's needs would always come first. Nothing would ever get in the way of her relationship with her precious daughter.

'Oh Ben,' she whispered, 'you never even knew about our lovely child. And what would you really have thought of my going out for an evening with another man?'

She tried to convince herself that he wouldn't have minded. That he wouldn't have wanted her to be lonely and unhappy.

Handsome, flirty Ben. She'd been the envy of the girls at the sailing club when they'd married and he'd become hers and hers alone. He would have been, often was, jealous if she'd chatted to any of the other men, but she'd never minded. It made her feel special and wanted.

It hadn't helped her to get over him, though. He'd tried to make her feel reliant on him all the time. She'd realised he'd wanted her to be something of a doormat, but her responsible job had prevented her from totally being in his shadow. Was she beginning to see that he may not have been the ideal man she'd always believed?

'Joe Meredith, what are you doing to me?' she whispered. He was making her think beyond tomorrow, that's what he was doing. It was wrong. Ben had been a wonderful man. A perfect husband. She'd always trusted him completely.

There was only one thing for it. She must stop seeing Joe, except at work, however difficult it would be. She would not, could not have any sort of relationship with him. The decision made, she went to bed and attempted to sleep.

The next few days were extremely busy and she scarcely saw Joe, which helped with her decision to stay away from him. She had the usual rounds of clinics and patients to go out to visit, including Sarah and her new baby.

Mother and child were thriving and Jamie, the toddler was very proud of his new sister.

Anna called in on Mrs Brierley.

'How's your husband getting on?' she asked.

'He's still in the hospital. They think they'll have to operate. It's all very difficult. We're so far from the hospital down here. Tell the truth, I'm that worried.'

'I'm sorry to hear that. Have you spoken to doctors at the hospital?'

'Don't say much do they? Can't really understand what they're talking about half the time.'

'I could ask Doctor Meredith to give you a call, once he's checked to see how your husband is.'

'Would you really? That would be wonderful. I don't like to bother him, though. Such a lovely young man, isn't he?'

'He's proving very popular with the patients. Don't worry. Your husband's in very good hands.'

As she drove away, Anna realised she had given herself a good excuse to speak to Joe again. Where had the 'keep him at arms length' resolution gone? Her mobile rang and she could see it was the surgery calling. She pulled over and answered it.

'Maggie here. Can you call on Mrs Pierce? Trewaddon Village? She's worried. Only six months into her pregnancy.'

'No problem. On my way. I'll be about

fifteen minutes.'

'Thanks Anna. I'll let her know you're on the way.'

She turned the car round and headed towards the little village. It was another isolated place high on the moors, a few miles outside Landris. She frowned. Sandy Pierce had been trying for a baby for several years without success until she'd finally become pregnant this time. She would be devastated if she lost this one and time was running out for her. She turned on to the minor road and saw a tractor ahead.

Anxiously, she hooted and the driver slowed right down and turned to look at the impatient person behind. He saw her blue uniform and recognised the car. He waved a hand before pulling into one side to let her pass. She wound down the window and called her thanks.

'No problem, nurse. Mrs Pierce is it?'

'That's right. Thanks again.'

Soon she was pulling up outside the cottage. She pushed open the door and called out.

'Mrs Pierce? Sandy? It's Anna.' It was dark inside after the bright sunlight and she took a moment to focus. Sandy was lying on the sofa looking very pale. 'It's all right. Just lie still.'

'Oh Anna, the baby will be OK, won't it?'

'Try to keep as calm as you can. Are you in pain?'

'Uncomfortable rather than a severe pain.

I'm not sure. I feel a bit sick.'

Anna took out her stethoscope. The foetal heartbeat was still there, faint but discernible. She took her temperature and blood pressure.

'The good news is that the baby's heartbeat's fine. Your blood pressure is a bit high, but that's understandable in the circumstances. I'm going to suggest we get you into the hospital for a scan and we'll see what they think about you staying in for a few days bed rest. Where's your husband?'

'He's at work. He's in an office in Trewin. He'll be that worried.'

'Well, I think it might ease your mind if we call him and suggest he meets us at the hospital. I'll phone for an ambulance. I could take you in my car but it's not a good idea. I want you to lie down flat for as long as possible. Don't worry. I'll let the surgery know where I am and I'll wait with you.'

Sandy was practically in tears as Anna made the arrangements. She packed a few things into a bag and picked up a personal CD player and some CDs. She saw some magazines on the side table and pushed them in too.

'Anything else you'd like? You may not have to stay in, but it's best to be prepared. Any pains?'

Sandy shook her head.

'Think I feel better now I know something's being done. I hope I'm not making a silly fuss. I hope too I'm not keeping you from

46

something important.'

'Nothing more important than making sure everything's all right for you. Now, shall I phone your husband or do you feel up to it?'

Anna followed the ambulance to the small local hospital at Landris. The maternity unit wasn't a large one, but it was popular with the locals. They wanted to have somewhere within easy reach and a place that wasn't one of the huge, anonymous hospitals many miles from home. Once her patient was settled, she left her with the hospital staff.

'I'll call and see you later,' she promised. 'And this looks like your husband coming in now. Hello, Jack. Sandy will be pleased to see you' Once she had reassured him that his wife was in good hands, she left them. Hopefully, a good spell of bed rest would enable them to keep their baby.

'I've had one thought. How would you feel about some acupuncture? It's evidently quite successful during pregnancy and I believe it can be relaxing. It's just an idea.'

'I'll do anything that might help,' Sandy said. 'I'm not sure about needles sticking in me though. Does it hurt?'

'I'm told it doesn't and I confess, I'm not sure how it works. Just that it does. I don't really know a great deal about it.'

'OK. Go for it. I'll try anything for this baby.'

'The problem is, I'm not sure the NHS will

cover the cost. I intend to ask about it but you may have to pay yourself this time.'

'As long as it doesn't break the bank, I'm willing to give it a go.'

'That's great. I'll be monitoring you at all times. I'll sort it out. Maybe when you get home again would be best.' She went out of the ward, pleased at the response to her suggestion.

'Hello. What are you doing here?' called a familiar voice. Joe was coming out of another ward.

'Patient of course. And you?'

'Just called in to see Mr Brierley. He's responding quite well but they'll definitely need to replace his heart valve. They'll have to take him to Truro of course, but he'll come back here afterwards.'

'Good diagnosis, Doctor Meredith. I saw his wife this morning. I'm afraid I promised you'd ring her to let her know what's going on. Hope you don't mind. Poor soul's worried sick and says she doesn't understand what the hospital doctors are telling her most of the time.'

'I was going to call round and let her know. She won't be able to visit him in Truro unless she can get a lift there. Maybe I'll try to organise something for her.'

'I hope you don't mean you'd drive her there yourself? Not strictly correct for a busy G.P.'

'And you always stick to the rules do you,

48

Midwife Kington?'

'Touché. Just don't get yourself involved or every patient will expect the same treatment. By the way, I wondered if you could put me in touch with your acupuncture practitioner. I have a patient who might benefit. She's here at the moment and wants to give it a try.'

'I doubt our esteemed senior partner would approve.'

'I'm planning to bring it up at the next meeting, but she's willing to pay herself. She's pretty desperate to keep a baby which seems to be giving problems.'

'I'll give you details when we get back to the centre. Gives me even more opportunity to spend time with you.'

'I haven't said thank you for last night. I really enjoyed it. Lovely meal. I was saying to Lucy, we should go there for lunch one day?'

'Good idea. How about next Saturday?'

'I meant I'd take her and Holly.'

'Even better. I can't wait to meet your little girl.'

'Hang on. I'm not sure that's such a good idea. Not yet. She's not used to having any men around and I don't want her to be confused.'

Joe's face fell and he looked puzzled. 'I'm not sure why not. But if that's what you want.' He turned away.

'Joe, I'm sorry. I didn't mean . . . oh heck. We could meet you there, if you like.'

'By a contrived accident, you mean? Chance meeting with a colleague. No thanks. Actually, I can't do it on Saturday anyhow. I've just remembered. Evie's invited us to a barbecue.'

'Us? As in you and me?'

'That's right.'

'But she doesn't know me. And isn't it a bit early in the year for barbecues?'

'Not indoor ones. We specialise in them. So how about it? Saturday? I can collect you about ten. Maybe have coffee with the delightful Aunt Lucy. Then I can meet Holly and the three of us can drive over to my sister's in time to help with lunch. Mind you, the boys are a bit rough. Will Holly cope with a five-year-old and a seven-year-old.'

'Slow down, Joe. You're way ahead of me. Evie's asked me and Holly to a barbecue when she doesn't even know me?'

'Organised it last night after I got back. I phoned her and told her I'd had dinner with the most gorgeous woman I've ever met and she immediately suggested, well insisted really, that we go over there. She can't wait to meet you. So, it's all settled?'

'Can I think about it?'

'Not for long. I'm going back to the surgery now. I'll meet you in half an hour. You can let me know then.' He whirled away and left her standing in the corridor looking totally bemused.

Joanne, the hospital midwife came out of

the ward.

'Anything wrong?' she asked her friend.

'Not really. I just feel as if I've been hit by a tornado. Have you met Doctor Meredith, our new locum?'

'I've seen him from a distance. Looks rather dishy to me. Wouldn't mind a closer look though?'

'He seems to be taking over my social life, suddenly.'

'Lucky you. Don't knock it. I could do with someone taking over mine. I usually manage to miss out on most things. Being a midwife tends to get in the way of much social life.'

'Tell me about it. Add on a toddler and that caps the lot.'

'Enjoy yourself anyway. I'm sure the doctor will have the right prescription for you.'

*   *   *

Anna arrived back at the surgery no clearer about her decision. Introducing Holly to Joe and meeting his family all seemed to be happening a bit too fast. They hardly knew each other and she wasn't prepared to risk upsetting her precious daughter. Ben would surely have hated her becoming involved with anyone else, however casual the relationship.

But, Ben wasn't here. Ben would never be here again and she had a lot of life ahead of her, with any luck. He couldn't, wouldn't expect her to live alone for ever. In her heart, she knew she probably would.

'Do you mind coming into my room?' Joe asked, almost the moment she entered the building. 'Well? Can I confirm the arrangements with Evie?'

'I . . . I haven't decided.'

'Right. That's a yes then.'

'But . . .'

'You need taking in hand. I shall volunteer for the task. You're much too indecisive. Time you lost that sad look and began to enjoy life as it should be enjoyed.'

'You are quite outrageous.'

'Prepare for an even greater outrage.' He took her fingers and kissed them gently. He pulled her closer and she felt herself leaning to him and his arms surrounded her. Her head fitted very comfortably into his shoulder. As swiftly as he had held her, he let go again. 'What do you think you're doing, nurse? Anyone could come in at any time.'

'Joe . . .' Her heart was thumping as she realised that she wanted to kiss him. She wanted to be held by him. He wasn't merely a replacement for Ben . . . he was someone else and she very much wanted to respond to him. 'Joe,' she managed to whisper, 'I think I'd love to come to meet Evie on Saturday.'

'Great. I'll order extra bangers immediately. Now, get on with you. I have work to do here. Anna?'

She turned and looked at him. His face was serious. 'I do very much want to kiss you. Kiss you properly,' he said softly. There was no laughter in his eyes as she spoke. No jokey line to cap his words. She felt her heart thud again. There was definitely some sort of magic between them. Maybe it was really only chemistry, but she felt there was a bit of magic in it too.

*   *   *

The rest of the day passed in a strange mixture of euphoria and trepidation. She'd agreed to accompany him on Saturday but all the time, she wondered if she were doing the right thing. It was rather soon to be meeting the family and also, for Holly to meet him. Everyone else thought it was a good thing that she should go out a bit more so she should stop beating herself up over whether it was right or wrong. But she found herself smiling every now and again at what was happening between them and the prospect of what might come.

Always the professional, the only difference her patients noticed was that she looked happy today. She called at the hospital and was relieved to find that Sandy was still holding on. The scan had seemed normal and they were advising complete rest for a few days. She was pleased that her own thoughts had been confirmed. When she finally arrived home, it was almost Holly's bedtime.

'I left her for you to bath,' Lucy said. 'I know you like to do it, even if it is a bit late.'

'No problem,' Anna said happily. 'Are you all right. You're looking tired again. Maybe Holly's too much for you to cope with. Perhaps we could get her into a playgroup a couple of mornings a week. What do you think? It would be good for her to mix with other children.'

'I'm fine, dear. Really. Just been overdoing it, I suspect. Now tell me, how was your day? And the lovely Doctor Meredith? Any comments about your evening out?'

'I had a good day on the whole. The usual round of things. One patient had to go into hospital but she's holding her own.'

'And . . . ?'

'And Doctor Meredith has asked me out at the weekend. With Holly. Hope you don't mind? He's invited us to meet his sister and family.'

'Of course I don't mind. But to meet his family? That's a bit soon, isn't it?'

'Perhaps it is. But I gather they're very close. Their parents died a long time ago and Evie sort of took over the role. She's only a couple of years older but I guess being a girl, she felt some responsibility. Anyway, it'll be nice for Holly to meet some new people. There are two boys for her to play with. It's all very casual.'

Lucy looked a bit dubious, but made no

comment. She sat down and put her feet up. It would be time enough to finish off the meal once Holly was in bed. She had mixed feelings at the thought of her niece going out with someone regularly. She would miss her and the little girl but she was sensible enough to know that Anna needed to find herself a new life. Besides, she might enjoy a little time to herself.

When Anna emerged from the bathroom, her uniform was sodden. She should have changed before she started the extremely soggy business of bathing her daughter. Still, it needed washing anyhow, so it wasn't a problem.

'More water,' Holly was yelling. 'More splashes.'

'No more. I'm too wet already,' she laughed, bundling the little girl into a towel. 'Now, let's get you dry and we'll see if Mr Teddy has kept your bed warm.' She dried her and pulled on a pink nightie. 'There now. Shall we say night, night to Lucy?' She carried her down and found Lucy fast asleep on the sofa. 'Let's leave her to sleep. Ssh. Night, night, Lucy,' she whispered and took Holly to bed. She read her a story and tucked her in.

Downstairs, Lucy hadn't stirred. Anna frowned. It was worrying. A couple of times recently Lucy had fallen asleep rather early and seemed lacking in energy. She hoped it wasn't symptomatic of some underlying problem. She needed to keep a careful watch over her aunt.

Anna went into the kitchen to see if there were any supper preparations to be done. There were two chops waiting to be grilled and potatoes peeled and left in water. She set to work and soon, there was an appetising smell coming from the kitchen. She peeped into the lounge but Lucy was still asleep. She wondered for a moment whether to leave her sleeping, but decided a meal was probably the best thing for her.

'Lucy,' she called softly, not wanting to wake her too suddenly. 'Supper's ready.'

'Oh heavens. How long have I been asleep? I'm so sorry. I should have cooked supper.'

'You'd got everything ready. Are you feeling all right?'

'Of course I am. Just needed a little snooze. I'm fine now. Must be getting old.'

CONCERNS OVER LUCY

It was horribly wet on Saturday when Joe came to collect them. He was dressed casually in jeans and T-shirt. The close fitting denims hugged his slim hips and emphasised the broad chest. She drew in her breath, wondering why such an attractive man was willing to spend a day with her and a toddler.

Anna had explained as much as one could explain to an almost three-year-old, that they were going to meet some new friends. When she introduced Joe, he put out a hand to be shaken and she solemnly took it, looking at her mother for approval as she did so.

'How do you do,' Joe said seriously.

'How do, do,' Holly replied and giggled. She held up her arms to be lifted and he did so. She stared at him and touched his chin. 'Fur. Like Mister Teddy,' she announced and giggled again.

'I should have shaved, shouldn't I? I didn't realise I would be subjected to such close scrutiny. This is my Saturday morning face. No shaves. No suit and tie.'

Anna watched the two of them together and smiled. There was an instant bond between them. Strange really, as her daughter had spent very little time with any males at all and was usually quite shy. Her colouring was very like Joe's. In fact, a casual stranger might think Holly was his own child. Joe became aware of her staring and raised an eyebrow.

'What? Why are you smiling. Just because I happen to have a very beautiful young lady in my arms, you're jealous, aren't you?'

'Hush,' she urged. 'What will Lucy think?'

'What will Lucy think about what?' her aunt asked as she came in with a tray of coffee. She stumbled slightly as she came in and Joe leapt to rescue the tray.

'Nothing. Just a little joke. You will have a good rest today, won't you?' Anna suggested.

'Of course I will. I might even do a bit of painting.'

'Don't you go clambering up a step ladder while you're in on your own,' Joe said seriously.

'Not that sort of painting. Canvas and small brushes only, I assure you.' She gave a giggle.

'That's a relief.'

'I must remember to make a dental appointment next week,' she said suddenly, right out of the blue.

'Have you got toothache?' Anna asked.

'Just a very sore mouth. I expect it's some sort of infection.'

'Shall I take a look?' Joe offered.

'Of course not. I'm fine. I shouldn't have mentioned it.'

'If you're sure,' Joe replied. He frowned slightly, but said nothing. 'Well now, are you

58

two ladies ready for the coming ordeal? Got your shin pads, elbow pads and protective head gear?'

'Goodness, what on earth are you planning?' Lucy asked in alarm.

'Just meeting my nephews. They're a rough bunch these Cornish folk. We'll see you later.'

'Take care, won't you, love?' Anna asked anxiously.

'Something wrong?' Joe asked as they were driving. Thoughtfully, he'd brought a child car seat and fixed it in the back so Anna was able to sit beside him in the front.

'I don't know. Lucy's been getting very tired lately. And her sudden need to see a dentist. That was very odd. I'm hoping it isn't a symptom of anything and that she's just been overdoing it a bit.'

'Who's her GP?'

'Well, Doctor Christopher actually.'

'So, maybe as I'm locum for him, I should take a look at her?'

'We'll see. She won't like me discussing her so we'll let her decide. But thanks. Now, where does this sister of yours live?'

'Not too far. In the middle of nowhere of course. Just too far for me to move in with them permanently. Mind you, we'd drive each other potty, I'm sure.'

*   *   *

Evie and Tim lived in what was once an old farmhouse. It was perched high on a hill with views of the sea and a large garden. Anna immediately took to Evie and knew they could grow to be good friends. The two boys were surprisingly gentle with Holly and despite all Joe's warnings, they were lovely children. It was too wet for them to play outside so Tom and Joe went off to supervise them while the women prepared the meal.

Evie was a pretty woman, probably a couple of years older than her brother. The family resemblance was clear and her two boys were absolute miniatures of their father. She was swathed in a large apron, but Anna noticed denim clad legs protruding beneath it and was relieved she'd made the right choice of clothes. She was so unused to going out, she felt self conscious about what she wore. Wearing her nurse's uniform so often had made her lazy.

'I haven't ever seen Joe this interested in a female before. I'm so pleased you could come and satisfy our curiosity,' she said with a laugh. 'I knew you must be someone special. He usually keeps everyone away from meeting us in case we put them off, is his usual excuse.'

'I've never met anyone quite like him. I'm never sure whether he's joking or serious. But, whatever else, he's a very good doctor, from what I've seen.'

Evie looked pleased and nodded her approval. 'I should think he is. He has such an

60

easy manner and seems able to explain things to people. I just wish he'd settle down and stay in one place for more than a few months. But, he's probably the proverbial rolling stone. He does like your practice though. Positively enthusiastic about it, for once. Makes a change as he usually suggests that most of the partners are ten years behind and blinkered. Perhaps it's something to do with the pretty midwife who also works there?' Anna blushed and shook her head. They hardly knew each other after all.

It was a lovely day. The meal was a great success with all the food being cooked on the indoor barbeque in one of the large barns with the door left open wide to let the smoke out. Holly ate everything with great enthusiasm, including a portion of usually hated salad. She insisted on sitting between her two new friends, Sam and Jake, who were remarkably tolerant of the little girl. She finally fell asleep as they drove back home, well past her bedtime.

'It's been such a lovely day. Thank you. Your sister and her family are wonderful. I've loved every minute of it.'

'And you're not put off me forever?'

'Joe, of course I'm not. Quite the opposite.' They stopped outside and he leaned over to her. He put his arm round her shoulders and very gently, kissed her lips. She moved towards him and he gave a deep sigh.

'Beautiful Anna. I've been wanting to do that all day.' She felt her senses reeling. She wanted it too.

'Holly might wake up.'

'So, are you going to invite me in?'

'Of course. But Lucy will be there.'

'Guess we have a problem, don't we? I'm living in a strange sort of bedsit at present. I tend to rent places wherever it's handy. This one certainly isn't the sort of place I could entertain a trendy midwife.'

'Trendy? Me?' she exclaimed with a loud laugh. Holly immediately woke up and began to whimper. 'It's OK, love. We're home now. You can have your bath and go straight to bed.'

'Joe, baff me. Joe read story,' she demanded.

'You've certainly made a hit with someone,' Anna laughed.

*   *   *

Anna was on duty the next morning and began her rounds early. She passed through Landris on her way to a patient and called in at the hospital to see Sandy Pierce.

'I'm hanging on in there,' she told Anna. 'They seem to think I should be all right as long as I don't do a thing and am waited on hand and foot. Don't know how long Jack will cope with it all.'

'I'm sure you'll manage. You might get someone to come in and clean for you once a week or even less. Jack can probably manage the washing at weekends. If you stay in bed most of the day, you can get up for a while in the evenings and spend the time together.'

'You make it sound easy.'

'It will be worth it. Now, I'd better get on. Sunday or not, there's the usual list of calls to be made. I'll see you again soon. Oh, I've been in touch with the acupuncturist. He says he can't make home visits because of some health and safety issue. Disposal of needles and insurance or something silly. So, you'll have to visit his clinic if you want to pursue it. He holds one in Trewin a couple of mornings a week.'

'That's great. Jack works there so I'm sure we can organise something.'

The rest of the day was spent on routine calls. The most important were the new babies who needed to be checked and the mothers reassured. She called at a family who had just produced baby number six. There was little the mother wanted to hear from the midwife and saw every visit by an official as some sort of spying.

'I'm not trying to catch you out, coming on a Sunday,' Anna assured her. 'I just want to make sure everything's OK and that baby's feeding properly?' She glanced round the small, untidy kitchen where three of the other children were clustered round the old range. There was washing up left in the sink and the remains of breakfast still on the table.

'Isn't there anyone who can help you?' she asked the weary woman.

'Course there ain't. He's gone down to meet his friends and I'm left 'ere with this lot.'

'Perhaps one of the older children could help you a bit. Just while the new baby's so small.'

'Fat chance.' The woman reached for a pack of cigarettes and Anna frowned.

'You shouldn't be smoking in front of the children, especially not near the baby. You know how bad it can be for them.'

'Mind yer own business. Now, if there's nothing else, I need to get on. You can see I've got plenty to do.'

It was pointless trying to do any observations on the mother while she was in this mood but at least she could ensure the baby was in reasonable health.

'I'd like to examine little . . . er, John,' she said looking at her notes to confirm the name. 'If that's all right.'

'Suit yourself. He's in the other room. Oh an' he's called Errol now. Me old man didn't like John. Thought it was too borin'.'

Dreading the conditions she might find, Anna pushed the door open and went to look for the baby. He was sleeping peacefully, a tiny thumb stuck in his mouth. Though not perfectly spotless, he was reasonably clean and certainly looked as if he was thriving. Gently, she lifted him from the ancient pram and unwrapped him from the shawl. She was aware of being looked at and turned to see the three children from the next room, standing in a row at the door watching.

'You've got a lovely little brother, haven't you?' No reply. She continued to examine him as he opened his eyes sleepily. 'You're beautiful, little one, aren't you?' His eyes opened wide and he gurgled gently. For only ten days old, he was remarkably alert. She looked in his nappy and saw that his bottom was rather sore. She took wipes from her bag and gently cleaned him and put some cream on the sore patches. 'Where does Mummy keep the clean nappies?' she asked.

'She's run out. Me dad's s'posed to be getting some but I s'pect he'll forget.'

'I've got one in my bag but we'll have to get some more. Baby John's bottom will be very sore if he isn't changed. Can you ask Mum to come in here, please?'

By the time she left, she felt reasonably content that things were as good as they could be. She was worried that the mother was doing too much, but she was as healthy as could be expected.

Feeling weary, she returned to the medical centre to write up her notes. With any luck, she could finish work early and get home to relieve Lucy of her daughter. She took out her keys to unlock the door and found it was already open. She punched in the weekend code for the inner door and looked to see who was on duty.

'Hello you.'

'Joe. What are you doing here? You're not down for duty are you?'

'I came to collect some notes and found a woman and her child knocking at the door. Little lad had cut himself on some glass and she thought he'd bleed to death. She didn't have a car and didn't think it was worth calling the ambulance as the surgery's in walking distance. I stitched him up and gave him a tetanus shot.'

'You shouldn't have to do that. Not on your day off. We can't win with some people. They go to the accident department at the hospital with their sore throats and such, to save making appointments. Then they come here with what are clearly potentially serious accidents.'

'It's no big deal, but I then decided I might as well do my notes here as take them to my depressing little bedsit. I suppose I should record the unexpected patient too or Doctor W. will be after me for the unauthorised use of a syringe and vaccine. How about you? What are you doing?'

'I've just finished for the day. I hate having to work Sundays but at least I get a day off later in the week. Got to write up the notes and then it's home. Give Lucy a break and maybe cook supper to save her the bother. Look, if you wanted to, you could come along. We usually have a roast on a Sunday, so there should be plenty.'

'Thanks a lot. That's great. How long do you need?'

'Half an hour. I'll give Lucy a call and warn her you're coming.'

She rushed to complete her notes, aware that her heart was singing at the thought of another evening in his company. Was she being pushy? If so, he didn't seem to mind. Besides, it would give him the opportunity to observe Lucy and see if he thought there really was anything wrong.

Both Lucy and Holly gave Joe a great welcome and Anna was happy to feel he could fit into their lives so easily. Whatever the future might bring, it was enough to share his company for the present. She was pleased that Lucy didn't mention his work for the lifeboats, as this still remained a huge hurdle to any sort of future they may consider.

'So, tell me why you are still a locum?' Lucy asked. 'What's wrong with settling down somewhere permanently?'

'Nothing at all. I haven't found anywhere that wants me. Or me it.'

'But you'd consider it if the right job came up?' Anna cringed. Her aunt was dropping hints the size of boulders and she felt uncomfortable.

'Would you like some more lamb?' she asked Joe, pointedly glaring at Lucy.

'Why not? I haven't had a meal like this in ages. Frozen dinners, tinned soup and beans are my usual fare.'

'Don't exaggerate. You eat with Evie and Tom most weekends. They told me.'

'Only when I'm not doing anything else.'

*   *   *

Once Holly was in bed, they sat chatting until Lucy announced that she was going to bed.

'But it's only half-past-eight,' Anna protested. 'You don't have to go on our account.'

'I'm feeling tired and in any case, I'm sure you have things you'd like to talk about.'

'I'm worried about you,' Anna remarked as casually as she could. 'You always seem to be tired at the moment.'

'I'm all right, dear. Course I'm all right. Now, where did I put my glasses? I have a good book and I might read for a little while. The milk bottles need putting out too. I'd better do that.' They heard a crash outside.

'I suspect that's one milk bottle less,' Anna remarked. 'I'd better help her clear up the broken glass. Excuse me, will you?'

Lucy pottered around for a while and at

last, went upstairs. A few moments later, she came down again. 'I'm sorry, I never said goodnight to you Joe, dear.'

'That's all right, Lucy. I never thanked you for a lovely meal. Sleep well. And if ever you need a check up, don't forget I'm standing in for Doctor Christopher so you can always ask to see me if you like.'

'Why should I want a check up? I don't think there's anything wrong, is there?'

'Not that I know of. But, if you are feeling extra tired, there may be some reason for it.'

'Nonsense. I'm just doing more than I've done for a while. Holly keeps me active and I'm just healthily tired. Now, I'll be off.'

They both said goodnight and sat down again. Joe took her hand and slipped his arm behind her. He leaned forward and kissed her. She sighed, realising how long she had missed the touch of another human.

Anna smiled. The unsuitability of this man and the total lack of any possible future together hit her. Was it so ridiculous that she wanted to like him?

'I'm sorry. I think I'd better wash up now or it will be left for Lucy to in the morning. I am a bit worried about giving her too much to do.' He kissed her fingertips and smiled at her.

'It's all right. I'll help. Won't take us long.'

'There's no need.'

They worked together companionably and the task was soon done. It also gave them a chance to talk more about Lucy's symptoms. He asked a few questions about her general health and a few more specific questions. Had she shown any signs of depression or loss of memory? Was her balance or walking affected in any way? She did seem to be dropping things, he observed.

Anna hadn't noticed but guiltily, she realised she had paid little attention to anything beyond Holly and her own work. She did intend to keep a better lookout for her aunt, but simply hadn't got round to it.

'Is there some reason for your questions? Is there something specific you have in mind?'

'Not really. Try to persuade her to come in for a check up though. As I said, we need to know if there is anything underlying her tiredness. I'll do some tests.'

Once the clearing up was finished, Joe decided he should leave.

'See you tomorrow,' she called as he walked away.

'Can't wait.'

She checked on her aunt and little daughter and then sat in front of the television, not really watching the costume drama that was showing. Her mind was racing over and over the same ground.

The picture of Ben on the mantelpiece stared down at her. She kept it there as a reminder to Holly of her daddy whom she had never known.

'I'M VERY SE...ed Holly the next
When Anna h...oth came down for
morning and ...ooking very pale and still
breakfast, Lu...ured coffee for them both
felt tired. A...l for Holly.
and put out... toast or cereal?' she asked her
'Do you...
aunt.
'Just ...fee, thanks. Sorry, but I feel quite
exhaus...d today.'

'I'm worried about you. You've been feeling tired for rather too many days lately. Why don't you call into the Medical Centre and get a check up? Just to be sure.'

'I'm fine, love. Don't worry. Probably need a rest or something.'

'I'll definitely take Holly to see Ben's parents next weekend. I'm not on call so it will be a good chance and you can have a complete rest for a couple of days. You could even go away for a bit of a break. Or why not go and stay at one of the hotels along the coast?'

'I'd be happier here. Might do some painting. If I still feel tired after that, I promise, I will make an appointment to see the doctor. Suppose it would be your Joe, I'd see wouldn't it? Is that allowed?'

'Why? Because you know him privately you mean? I don't see it's a problem. Are you sure

For once, the sight of his familiar face didn't make her cry. She did manage several large pangs of guilt. How could she still be grieving over her loss and still want someone else?

Joe Meredith. What was he doing to her? Breaking down her resolve, that was what he was doing. She needed to be very sure of him before she allowed anything more to happen. He seemed ideal in so many ways. But so much depended on his own future plans. And there was still the unsolved problem of the lifeboats. Sailing and the sea had already robbed her of her happiness once.

'I'M VERY SERIOUS ABOUT YOU.'

When Anna had dressed Holly the next morning and they both came down for breakfast, Lucy was looking very pale and still felt tired. Anna poured coffee for them both and put out cereal for Holly.

'Do you want toast or cereal?' she asked her aunt.

'Just coffee, thanks. Sorry, but I feel quite exhausted today.'

'I'm worried about you. You've been feeling tired for rather too many days lately. Why don't you call into the Medical Centre and get a check up? Just to be sure.'

'I'm fine, love. Don't worry. Probably need a rest or something.'

'I'll definitely take Holly to see Ben's parents next weekend. I'm not on call so it will be a good chance and you can have a complete rest for a couple of days. You could even go away for a bit of a break. Or why not go and stay at one of the hotels along the coast?'

'I'd be happier here. Might do some painting. If I still feel tired after that, I promise, I will make an appointment to see the doctor. Suppose it would be your Joe, I'd see wouldn't it? Is that allowed?'

'Why? Because you know him privately you mean? I don't see it's a problem. Are you sure you're going to manage Holly today?'

'I'll be fine. We can have a quiet day at home.'

Anna didn't really have a choice and left the two of them finishing breakfast and with a promise that Lucy would phone if there was anything wrong. It was her morning for the ante-natal check-ups and there were already a couple of her patients waiting for her when she arrived. The women who lived locally usually visited the centre for their checks and Anna drove out to those who lived sonic distance away and who either had other small children or no transport. It was a large village and there were a number of young families.

It was a routine clinic, with all except one of her patients turning up. She wrote up all the notes and phoned Landris Hospital to see how Mrs Pierce was doing. All was still well and they planned to discharge her in a couple of days. When she went to ask on Reception about her patient who hadn't arrived, Maggie offered to phone and see why the mother-to-be had failed to keep the appointment. She reported back to Anna.

'Seems she had someone coming to fix the washer and as she has three kids already, didn't think it was important to get a check up. And before you ask, she hadn't realised she needed to let us know about cancelling the appointment.'

'I suppose she'd better go on my list for a

home visit later in the week. Her blood pressure needs checking and I could do with seeing if she'd made arrangements for the rest of the children to be looked after, when the new one arrives.'

'So, how's it going with the gorgeous Doctor Meredith?' Maggie asked.

Anna coloured slightly. 'He seems to be getting on well. Popular with the patients, from what I gather.'

'Wasn't what I meant and well you know it? You've seen him a few times, haven't you?'

'The bush telegraph had been working overtime, has it?'

'So? What's the news?'

'There isn't any. Is he in this morning by the way? There's something I need to ask him.'

'He's still out but due back for the meeting at lunch time. You hadn't forgotten it, had you?'

'Course not,' she lied. She had forgotten it of course, having planned to dash home to check on Lucy. Besides, she hadn't packed any sandwiches so it gave her an excuse. Lucy hadn't been capable of doing anything extra this morning. Still, she could always phone. They usually had sandwiches brought in for the staff on the days they had practice meetings.

She went back to her room and called Lucy. Her aunt claimed that she was feeling fine and that Anna mustn't worry. Having five minutes

74

to spare, she used her own mobile to call Ben's parents. Mrs Kington seemed pleased enough at the thought of seeing her granddaughter at the weekend but was not exactly welcoming.

'It's so long since we saw you. I expect I shall scarcely recognise Holly. What time will you get here?' she asked in her rather slow manner.

'I'll start off as soon as I finish work. Probably get to you about seven.'

'We usually eat at six. And won't it be a bit late for Holly?'

'It's the best I can do. I don't want to drive out of Cornwall on Saturday morning. The traffic's usually awful. We can always eat before we leave if it's a problem.'

Anna was switching off her phone as Joe tapped at the door and peered round to see if she was on her own.

'Good morning. And how are you today? Recovered from the overdose of Meredith company over the weekend?'

'I'm OK. Just suffering from the usual lack of enthusiasm from Ben's mother. I suggested I take Holly to see them for the weekend but her reaction was somewhat negative.'

'Don't go then. Spend it with me instead.'

'I'd love to, but I do feel duty bound to make sure the Kingtons know their granddaughter. Besides, Lucy really needs a bit of a break. She's agreed to come and see you if she's still tired after a weekend on her

75

own, by the way.'

'Fair enough. Hope she does come. I'm a bit concerned about her. Try to persuade her. And if you change your mind about going away, we could always go somewhere ourselves. Couple of days in some nice quiet hotel.'

'Joe, please. It sounds wonderful but . . .'

'But nothing. My unfortunate sense of humour comes as part of the whole weekend package.'

Anna couldn't help but laugh. 'Are you ever serious?'

'Only when strictly necessary.' His grin faded. 'But I'm very serious about you. Still, I can wait. Good for the soul to be denied what you want most in the world and wait until the time is right. And believe me, Anna Kington, that time will come.' He leaned over her desk and planted a kiss on her forehead before swinging out of the room. He turned again.

*   *   *

The practice meeting was more enjoyable than usual, sitting next to Joe. He obviously felt the same way about her and well, it seemed very silly to deny herself the undoubted pleasure of his company. She dragged her mind back to Doctor Whittaker's words.

'Now we come to the most important subject on today's agenda. As you all know,

Doctor Christopher is on sabbatical for a total of three months and Doctor Meredith is replacing him as locum. When those three months are up, I understand that Jim Christopher is planning to take up further research and wants greatly reduced hours here. With everyone's agreement, I'd like to offer Joe an extension to the original three months, assuming of course, he is willing to stay.'

Anna felt herself blushing once more. Joe hadn't mentioned this proposal at all, assuming he actually knew about it in advance.

'Well, Joe, any thoughts?'

'I don't know . . . I hadn't thought . . . I mean . . . But thanks for the vote of confidence. I can't be all bad or you'd be wanting me to pack my bags. Can I have a day or two to think about it?'

'Of course. But I'm sure we'd all be in favour of an extension for Doctor Meredith, wouldn't we?'

There was a murmur of assent around the table. Joe looked pleased. Even though it was only a few months longer, it meant he'd be around for a while yet, assuming he accepted the offer.

'I'd like to raise something,' Anna said when there was a momentary break. 'Sorry I didn't put it on the agenda but I didn't have time. The thing is, there's been a lot of research recently into using complementary medicine in the NHS.'

'Oh come now, Anna. Aromatherapy, you mean?'

'I wasn't thinking about aromatherapy,' she said with a hint of mockery. 'Though I hear it helps with relaxation quite a lot. I was actually considering the use of acupuncture during pregnancy and childbirth. There have been some very positive reports, and well, I'd like to consider using it here.'

'I agree,' Joe joined in. 'I know a practitioner who had studied in China where it's used in all the major hospitals.'

'Far too expensive and it isn't proven,' Doctor Whittaker said dismissively.

'But can't we at least consider it?' Anna suggested.

'It saves on the cost of pain relief, actually,' Joe added. 'So it needn't increase budget costs by very much if at all.'

'Let me have figures. I'll look at them.'

The meeting rolled on until it was almost two o'clock. Appointments re-started at two fifteen, so the meeting was called to a halt.

'That was a bit of surprise, wasn't it?' Joe remarked as they went back along the corridor to their own rooms. 'Fancy someone wanting me to stay on a bit longer. Most unusual. Mostly they can't wait to get rid of me.'

'Didn't you know about it?'

'Course I didn't. I would have mentioned it to you. I'd have liked to be told before, really.

Save me looking as if I can't string words together properly. How would you feel about it?'

'I'd be delighted. Save me feeling pressured.'

'Sorry? How do you mean, pressured?'

'I don't have to make any rushed decisions before you disappear again.' He stared at her curiously but said nothing.

'Exactly what sort of decisions?'

She blushed and looked away. Perhaps she was jumping the gun. Making assumptions. 'I'd better get on with my work. I have several calls to make and I need to get home early tonight. Thanks for the support by the way. About the acupuncture?'

'I suspect we'll have a fight on our hands. But one has to keep trying. Maybe they'll change their minds over offering me an extension. But, if it helps with your decisions . . . whatever they are.'

He turned and left her office. She swore quietly to herself. Had she mistaken Joe's intentions? Was she making too much of his odd comments? She forced her mind back to her work and made herself concentrate for the rest of the afternoon. She managed to finish the last of her visits early and called Maggie to let her know she was going straight home and would finish the paperwork there. She was still anxious about her aunt and wanted to try and take some of her workload.

*   *   *

'How are you feeling?' she asked Lucy when she arrived home later that day.

'Much better thanks, dear,' she replied.

They spent a happy evening together and indeed, Lucy did seem less tired.

'I phoned Ben's mother and we're going on Friday evening. She didn't sound very pleased about it but we're going anyhow. Oh and Joe's been asked to stay on at the practice for a further period.'

'Oh, my dear, that's lovely. I expect you're pleased, aren't you?'

'To tell the truth, I'm not sure. I thought I was, but he seemed a bit strange about it. He hasn't actually said yes, as far as I know. Said he wanted to think about it.'

'Gives you more time to get to know him.'

'Maybe. Now, an early night for you,' Anna told her aunt. 'I'll bring you some hot chocolate to bed if you'd like that.'

'You're getting very bossy, young lady. But you're right as usual. An early night is a good idea.'

*   *   *

The rest of the week flew by. She was on call on Thursday night, hoping for a quiet night before her journey on Friday. No such luck.

80

She was called out around ten o'clock to a lady having a third child, who had begun labour earlier in the evening. They badly wanted a home birth and had waited for as long as they could before calling. The two older children were in bed and settled so the house was quiet. Madeleine was well prepared with everything ready, as she had been told.

Anna listened to the baby's heart and was satisfied that all was well for the moment. A little later, she attached the portable monitor and examined her patient again. She frowned slightly. The baby was almost ready to be born but the monitor showed the baby's heartbeat was erratic. It was beginning to show signs of distress. She thought the mother was probably going to need help. She could really do with another pair of hands, but she knew the other midwife was busy elsewhere.

'Excuse me a moment,' she said and left the room. She pulled out her mobile phone and dialled the out of hour's number of the practice.

'Hi. I'm going to need the duty doctor to come to assist with a home birth. Quickly please.' She gave the address and left the operator to organise everything.

'Is there something wrong?' the father asked anxiously when she returned.

'Nothing to worry about. I just need some extra help. I'd like the doctor to be here too. I don't want to prolong the labour and this should help. Besides, an extra pair of hands is always useful.'

Minutes later, the doorbell rang and Joe came into the bedroom.

'Hello there,' he said cheerfully. 'How's it going?'

'I'd like you to assist, please. The baby's beginning to show signs of distress but Madeleine here is doing a fine job.' Her professionalism allowed her to continue to work calmly and efficiently though she was certain her heart rate had accelerated considerably. Joe slipped off his jacket and tie. He examined the patient and nodded. 'I'll give you an injection now to stop the pain.'

Madeleine nodded.

'Exactly what's happening?' asked the father. 'I don't understand. She was doing so well and she's had two babies already.'

'Nothing to worry about. The baby's having a bit of a problem making his way into the world. Maybe he or she's a larger baby than the others.'

Anna was giving a local anaesthetic while she was explaining. Joe was putting on a gown and opened the sterile pack with the equipment they would need.

Eventually after one more hefty push the baby was born. Anna clamped the cord and gave the scissors to the father to cut it, nodding encouragement.

'Wow,' he breathed. 'Thank you so much.'

His hands shook as he did it.

'What's going on?' asked a little voice from the doorway. 'Who're all these people?' Davy, the oldest child, was standing with thumb in mouth.

'You've got a new little sister,' his daddy told him. 'Come and look.'

Davy came closer and stared. 'She hasn't got any hair. And she's a bit grubby. I thought babies had to be kept clean.'

'She's still very new,' Anna told him. 'I'm going to wash her in a minute. Would you like to help me?'

'No thanks. I'm going to fetch James.' He went into their bedroom and they could hear him trying to wake his little brother. 'James come and see. James. Wake up. We've got a sister. There's people here, who brought her.'

Two small pyjama-clad boys stood in the doorway.

'Come and look,' their mother invited. Hand in hand they approached the bed and looked at the tiny bundle. The baby made tiny noises and they giggled.

'She's a bit little. And not much like a girl.'

'There's a present for each of you on the table. A welcome from the new baby.' The pair scampered across the room and ripped off the pretty paper from the two packages.

'Now it's time you went back to bed. You can see her tomorrow and play with your new toys then.' Their dad hustled them off to bed and Joe and Anna completed their tasks.

'Can I get you a drink?' the father asked.

'Love a cup of tea,' they all said together.

Outside the house, some time later, Anna and Joe stood by their cars.

'You did a good job there,' Joe said. 'In fact, you're very good. Wasn't it magic? Though you're probably so used to it, it doesn't mean so much any more.'

'Don't you believe it! I always feel like it's the first time with every one. Thank you for not trying to take over. I appreciate it.'

'I'm not even sure you needed me but I'm so glad to share it. I don't see nearly enough of new lives. I seem to be bogged down with poor folk near the end of their lives. Especially here in Cornwall. Everyone's favourite place to retire. Thank you, Anna.'

'And I noticed no jokes or anything. Is this the professional you I still don't know?'

'Absolutely. Never joke when anything's that serious. You still going away this weekend?'

'Yes. Tomorrow . . . today, after I finish. Wish me luck.'

'You wish me luck too. I'm on duty this weekend. Thought I might as well volunteer, as you weren't going to be around.'

'That's taking it a bit far, isn't it? Who's the lucky doctor to be let off weekend duties?'

'I don't mean here. Lifeboat duty. I haven't done it for ages as I've been kept to busy.'

Anna felt her heart plummet. She'd almost

forgotten about his other activities.

'Just make sure you don't take any risks,' she said with a tremor.

'I can't promise that. But I'm glad you care. Now, home with you. You need some sleep.'

Though she'd known Joe would be facing lifeboat duties at some point, she had pushed the thought away. She would be thinking about him on and off all weekend. Thinking about the all-powerful sea and the fact that men would be risking their own lives to save people who often disregarded safety warnings. She shuddered at the thought of water closing over someone . . . someone drowning. Would she ever be free of the visions?

JOE MAKES A PROPOSITION

It was a tedious weekend. Ben's parents were clearly still resentful of the fact that Anna hadn't alerted the rescue services earlier. She had told them over and over again her reasons, but they didn't want to listen. She finally told them about Joe who had been part of the team and his suggestion that nothing more would have helped. Nor did they want to accept his theory that the boat had gone down instantly, before Ben could have sent a distress message.

'Ben was much too careful for that. He had all the best equipment on board. He must have been taken ill or something. You're medically trained, couldn't you see he was not well before he set out?' Anna could hardly believe what she was hearing. This was a new tack. It was now her fault for failing to diagnose some terminal illness.

'I think I'll take Holly out for some fresh air. We'll go and play outside for a while.'

'Don't let her go on the flowerbeds, will you, dear? The bulbs are just coming up and we don't want them to be damaged.'

The whole place was a child nightmare, Anna decided. Cut glass knick-knacks on every table. Priceless china left on shelves, well within the reach of the curious toddler. Kitchen cupboards with every sort of cleaning material known to man, all easily available.

*　　　*　　　*

By Sunday morning, Anna was more than ready to be off. How much she had wished she'd taken up Joe's offer of a weekend away with him. She blushed slightly, glad that neither of her in-laws were in the least bit psychic.

'I won't leave too late. Lucy has been under the weather recently and I'm anxious to know how she is,' she told her in-laws at breakfast.

'You can't possibly leave before lunch. We've got a roast specially. We know how much Ben loved his Sunday lunches.' It must have been the hundredth reference to what Ben liked or didn't.

'Thank you. We'll get off straight after lunch, though.'

Neither of them showed much interest in playing with their granddaughter and seemed more concerned with keeping everywhere straight and clean and the garden tidy. Over lunch, Anna was amazed when they suddenly offered to keep Holly to stay for a week or two.

'If your aunt is finding her too much, perhaps she could stay here. We'd like to have her to ourselves for a while.' Anna's mouth dropped open in sheer amazement. Let Holly stay here? Without her? Never.

87

'I couldn't possibly. But thank you for the offer. We haven't brought enough clothes or toys and she's quite energetic. You'd be worn out with her in no time.'

'We hardly know her,' Ben's mother complained. 'And she hardly knows us.'

'I'm afraid I think she's too young to be in a strange environment without her mummy for several days.'

'I think you're being very selfish. You deprive us of our only son and then refuse to let his child stay with us. You farm her out every day with that aunt of yours and yet her own grandparents don't get a look in.'

Anna was ready to explode but Mr Kington interrupted. 'Now dear, don't get upset,' her father-in-law said soothingly, his arm around his wife's shoulders. 'You know it isn't good for your poor heart. I'm sure Anna will bring Holly to stay for longer next time. And you can't entirely blame her for Ben's death. He was the one who sailed off, after all.' Anna looked at him, grateful for the support, however half-hearted it may have sounded.

'But she's got all the benefits afterwards. His life insurance and that lovely house. I couldn't believe you'd want to sell it. The home you made together.'

'You don't know anything,' Anna burst out, angry at the harsh words. 'If you want the truth, Ben had cleared out all our money from the bank and he'd stopped paying for the life insurance. He'd even taken out a second mortgage without telling me. I had to sell our lovely home because your son had got into such terrible debt. I still haven't finished paying off all of it. There was nothing from any policies. If it hadn't been for the generosity of my aunt, we'd have been on the streets. None of it has been easy at all. Now, if you'll excuse me, I'll go and pack our things into the car. Keep an eye on Holly, please.'

'But Mother's heart isn't strong. Please don't upset her this way. I can understand you are worried but I can't have you endangering her life.'

'Good job I'm not leaving Holly to stay then, isn't it?' She paused. 'What's wrong with Mrs Kington's heart anyway?'

'It's been broken . . . by Ben's untimely death.'

'That's rubbish,' she said without thinking.

'The strain of it has made her ill. She's never recovered. Seeing you brings it all back.'

'It's been tough for us all. I've had rather a lot to cope with myself. It isn't easy bringing up a child and having to work as well. Now, if you'll excuse me, I'll remove the cause of such stress from your house right away.'

She couldn't remember ever feeling so angry before. It was so unfair. Ben could never do any wrong in his mother's eyes and usually, his father wasn't much better. She'd only come to see them out of guilt. This was possibly the last place on earth she wanted to be. As for them having Holly to stay for a couple of weeks, the poor child wouldn't know what had hit her. She'd have to be a lot older before she would even consider leaving her precious daughter with these people, grandparents or no.

'Thanks for a nice weekend,' she managed to mumble as she strapped Holly into the car seat.

'We've enjoyed having you,' her father-in-law replied. 'And don't take any notice of what Mother said. She really is still grieving for Ben.'

'Aren't we all?'

'If you really are in financial difficulties, I'm sure we could help.'

'Thank you, but I'll manage. I've managed so far.' She wouldn't take a penny from them. She tried to quell the seething anger as she drove home and sang songs to her little girl as they drove. Holly squealed with delight as she joined in with the few words she knew. They were nearing home when her phone rang. She put the earplug in and pressed the button. The screen said it was Lucy calling.

'Hello, Lucy?'

'Anna. It's Joe. Where are you?'

'Just about to leave the A30. About half an hour away. What are you doing there? Is something wrong?'

'It's OK. I'm at your aunt's house. She isn't

well and I'm insisting on taking her into hospital. She needs some tests. No need to panic.'

'I'll meet you at the hospital. It'll be quicker.'

'What about Holly?'

'I'll sort something. What's wrong with Lucy?'

'Don't know yet. Better go. See you soon. And don't worry.'

Don't worry, Anna thought. Ridiculous statement. How could she not worry? Poor Lucy. She should have known it was something serious. She took several deep breaths and made herself calm down. After the scene with her mother-in-law, and now this, it needed all her self-control.

*   *   *

When she arrived at the small hospital, the car park was packed solid, as usual. She found a space in a nearby street and lifting Holly on to her hip, she almost ran to the Admissions Department. She found Joe and almost fell into his arms. He was so dependable, so strong, she thought. The sort of person everyone needed as part of their lives.

'Hey, it's all right. I've got her into the cubicle and the doctor's with her now. They're taking some blood tests and I'm sure they'll come up with the right answer.'

'But how did you get involved. Did Lucy phone you? She must have felt really bad to phone you.'

'She didn't. I happened to be passing and called in to see if you were back. She looked terrible, so I examined her and decided we needed to do something urgently. You can see her in a minute. But, are you all right? You look very flustered. Let me take Holly. Come here, little one. You're a bit of a lump for your mummy to carry, aren't you?'

'Lo, Joe,' she said, snuggling against him happily.

'I had a blazing row with Ben's parents, which upset me no end. Then this happens. Apart from all the worry about poor Lucy, what on earth am I going to do?'

The full impact of Lucy being ill hit her and she felt tears pricking her eyes. She relied on Lucy for everything. How was she going to do her job?

'Mrs Kington? You can come in to see your aunt now.'

It felt strange to be on the other side of the fence, a visitor rather than staff. The doctor pushed open the curtains and almost trembling with fear, Anna went into the cubicle.

'I'm so sorry, love,' her aunt said immediately. 'I don't quite know what's happening. When Joe called in, I was feeling rather dizzy and he just took over. Organised

92

everything.'

'I'm so glad he did. You're in the right place. I'm only sorry I wasn't here for you. I should never have gone away and left you alone.'

'Don't be silly, dear. You did it for the best. They'll soon sort me out, I'm sure. Where's Holly?'

'With Joe. She's fine. A bit tired perhaps.'

'He's a good man.'

'Do you know what might be wrong?' she asked the doctor who was still hovering around.

'We'll know more tomorrow when we have the test results.'

'I see. Is there anything you need, Lucy?'

'I'm fine. Joe collected the essentials for me before we left. You go home now. Get Holly to bed. She must be worn out, poor little thing. And you try to get some sleep. I'll soon be home, so you won't have to worry about anything. Perhaps you can get the day off tomorrow?'

'Don't worry. I'll manage something,' Anna said, trying to sound convincing.

*　　　*　　　*

Joe insisted on accompanying her home and helping to put Holly to bed. She unpacked the car and sat staring at the suitcase. Joe handed her a glass of wine.

'Drink this. Supper's on the way.'

'I can't each much,' she protested.

'Well tough. You can watch me eat.'

'I don't understand. You haven't had time to cook anything. I don't even know what's in the fridge.'

'Nor do I. There's a pizza being delivered at any moment.'

'Now there's efficiency. I forgot. How was your duty stint with the lifeboat?' She didn't really want to think about it but forced herself to try to be unemotional about it.

'Fine. Several early holidaymakers with suicidal tendencies. Why on earth people don't read notices, I'll never understand. When it says no bathing, that's what it means. All these clever clogs who think they can swim against currents they can't even see.'

The doorbell rang and the pizza arrived. Despite her thoughts of not wanting to eat, it smelt so appetising that she tucked in hungrily. Joe cleared up the majority of it and they sat back feeling almost relaxed. Anna frowned, worried about her aunt, comforted by Joe's presence.

'I've got a proposition,' Joe said after a short while. 'How about I move in here with you and then I can help out with Holly? We can arrange our shifts a bit so if you're on nights, I'll be here and vice versa. We can probably organise a bit of leeway during the day too. And with a few mornings at playgroup, problem sorted.'

'I couldn't impose. Besides, what would everyone think?'

'There's a spare bedroom. So no need to panic. You can even lock your door if you're worried.'

'I don't mean that. It's wonderfully kind of you. But I can't interfere with your life like that.'

'You must realise you're already interfering with my life. In fact, you've pretty much turned my plans upside down, just by being you.'

'I'm not sure.'

'Trust me, I'd like to help.' His face took on a serious expression and he touched her hand. 'Don't worry.'

'But it's my problem.'

'Fine. I'm going to collect a few things from my dreary bedsit now. And while I'm away, you can put some sheets on that bed. You need to have a few decisions made for you. No. Don't say anything more. I'll be back in half an hour.'

Anna's emotions were running riot for almost the entire half hour he was away. Maybe it would work and after all, it was only a very temporary situation. Chances were, Lucy would be home again in a day or so. Perhaps she would be able to sign on for more nights and free her daytime hours to be with her daughter.

If either Joe or Lucy were to stay home with Holly at nights, she could probably carry on working normally. Her colleagues would probably jump at the chance for a spell of nights without duty. She grabbed clean sheets from the airing cupboard and made up the spare bed. She put out fresh towels and tidied a few things away that had been dumped in the usually unused room.

The doorbell rang. She would have to find him a key, she realised. And did he eat a cooked breakfast or just toast, like they did? She really knew nothing about this man who was about to share their home.

'I've emptied my fridge and brought anything that was useful. Hope you don't mind, only I hate wasting anything.'

'Of course not. Make yourself at home. I've put clean sheets out and towels. Oh and I'll find you a key . . .' She was babbling on and she realised. 'There's a spare one in a pot in the kitchen.'

'Relax, Anna. This is supposed to help you, not send you into overdrive in organising. Once I've taken my stuff up, we'll make some plans.'

*　　　*　　　*

They spent the rest of the evening deciding the best course of action. She mentioned her idea of working nights, which he agreed with, but was concerned that she would soon be overtired, especially if she was looking after

96

Holly all day.

Whatever happened, she needed to take the next day off. They'd just have to manage without her at the medical centre.

'But you do realise that I'll have to give them this number as my contact number,' he pointed out. 'I'll do my best to preserve your reputation intact.' He gave her a weak grin.

*   *   *

She lay awake, aware that Joe was lying only a few feet away. She felt comforted by his presence in the house. She was also slightly disturbed at having him so close. She felt confused. She knew she had deep-rooted fears about any relationship and specific fears about any future with Joe. He was always teasing and flirted with her but he seemed not to want anything more.

Then she began to go through a period of remorse. She was being selfish. Poor Lucy was ill in hospital and they had no idea what was wrong. How could she be thinking of herself and not her beloved aunt's welfare?

'I'll get into work early today and make sure everyone knows you won't be in,' Joe said. 'I expect you'll want to go to the hospital first thing. You could try at the nursery and see if they can take Holly. Under the circumstances, they're usually willing to help out.'

'Good idea. I'll phone after breakfast. What

do you want to eat for breakfast? I'm not sure what's in the fridge.'

'Coffee and toast would be a great improvement on my usual fare.'

*   *   *

Lucy was in the Admissions Ward and sitting up in bed, looking rather frail. 'Hello dear,' she said with false brightness. 'How on earth have you managed to come in at this time? Shouldn't you be at work? And where's our little girl?'

'I'm taking the day off and Holly's gone to nursery school. She seemed delighted to see a whole lot of new toys and all the other children. I'm collecting her at twelve. Now, any news yet?'

'I don't really understand what they're talking about. Some sort of anaemia, they think. That's easy though, isn't it? Just take iron pills.'

'Well, maybe. I'm not sure. You seem to be rather unwell for just plain anaemia. I'd like to talk to the doctors, if you don't mind. See what they say.' Lucy nodded her agreement and Anna went in search of the doctor in charge of her aunt.

He said that he wasn't yet certain of a diagnosis and said that he wanted to keep her in for a few days and carry out more stringent tests. He seemed unwilling to talk much about her aunt, more than the usual patient confidentiality.

She suspected that Lucy had been trying to keep any worries from her and asked the doctor not to tell her too much. But it worked the other way round. She was already beginning to believe it was something far more serious and that everyone was trying to spare her feelings. Instead, she became more worried than ever. She fully intended talking to Joe later. She had to know what she was facing.

After the hospital visit, she went to collect Holly and called in at the Medical Centre. Everyone was most sympathetic and willing to help wherever possible. Doctor Whittaker suggested they might share with the hospital for extra cover and at Anna's suggestion of taking on extra night duties, he thought they might be able to liaise with the Maternity Department at Landris.

'As a matter of fact, we're considering a plan to integrate the midwifery service with all the local practices and the hospital. Much more efficient.'

'Maybe efficient, but I'd hate it to become such a large organisation that individual patient care could be compromised,' she retorted.

'Efficiency, my dear. We all have to look at greater efficiency.'

Anna began to wonder how soon he was

likely to retire. All the same, she needed his support at this time and could not afford to antagonise him. The midwife teams usually worked together in any case, so it was a case of a little more organisation. If she did work more at the hospital, it looked as if it might work out well. Her grand plans for introducing more complementary therapies would have to be left on hold. She hoped that there were no emergencies among her special patients the next few weeks, particularly those planning home births.

*   *   *

When Joe came home that evening, she had prepared a casserole for supper. Holly was delighted to see him and hopped round squeaking his name over and over.

'Luv Joe,' she said as she cuddled Mister Teddy at bedtime.

'That's nice,' Anna said, suddenly feeling deep concern. Joe was becoming an integral part of their lives. Perhaps a bit too important to the little girl.

'This is great,' he said appreciatively as he cleared his plate. 'I could get used to this. Oh, I made some notes for you after the meeting today. Most people seemed remarkably enthusiastic that I said I'd probably stay, by the way. Asked if it was anything to do with the fact I've moved in here.'

'You didn't announce it at the meeting, did you? Surely not. I'll never dare look anyone in the face again.'

'Of course not. I was only teasing. The main subject that came up was after-hours cover. Have you heard about it?'

'Not a thing. Unless you mean the stuff on the news?'

'It's all a bit complicated. Tied in with salaries and such. Working conditions. You know the sort of stuff.'

'I suppose the good thing would be that doctors don't have to work so many long hours. It must impair performance if you're too tired.'

'Which is precisely why I'm worried about you and your intended plans.'

'I'm fine. But, can you tell me what you know about this anaemia that Lucy's suffering from? It's clearly a lot more than ordinary anaemia. She seems to think a few iron pills and she'll be fine.'

'She's asked me not to tell you anything to worry you. Patient confidentiality and all that.'

'You'd better tell me. I'm already worried sick. Is it leukaemia?'

'No, I don't think so. All right, but don't blame me if Lucy never speaks to me again. We think she may have pernicious anaemia. It will be confirmed by doing a bone marrow test. She'll also have to have a series of tests to see why she isn't absorbing folic acid.'

101

'But why should it happen now?'

'She's reached a point where the deficiency has become significant. It's no good just pouring the missing vitamin into her if she can't absorb it.'

'So this is probably going to take some time?'

'Possibly. I wondered about when I asked about her memory loss and whether she was less sure on her feet.'

'Goodness. You noticed all that just over a meal and I live with her and never even thought about it. I feel ashamed.'

'No need to feel that. I was able to be more objective and I've seen it before. A distant cousin of my parents had it so I knew the signs to look for. It isn't in your area of expertise anyhow. One often thinks of anaemia or some viral infection when someone complains of perpetual tiredness. Look, changing the subject. I've been thinking about something.'

'Oh?' Anna wondered what on earth was coming next.

'About acupuncture.'

'Acupuncture?'

'Yes. If you are going to recommend it, even prescribe it in time, you should try it yourself.'

'But there's nothing wrong with me.'

'There doesn't have to be. I think it would be a good experience and it would certainly help with the stress you're under. I'll make you an appointment and you can go at the end of work one day soon. I can come home to be with Holly, before you go on your shift.'

'OK. Thanks, Joe. I must say I'm intrigued about the whole thing. I've no idea how it works, but I'd love to give it a go. Mind you, the timing isn't good. I'm rushing round like a mad thing.'

'So an hour's relaxation will do you good.'

*   *   *

While Holly went to nursery for the next few mornings, Anna tried to get some sleep. Luckily, Holly had taken to it with great enthusiasm and under the circumstances, the organisers were happy to have her there. The constant night shifts were taking their toll and Anna was already finding the change in routine quite difficult to cope with.

Sleeping during the day seemed all wrong. Some nights were relatively peaceful but then there would be one night when the particular baby took forever to arrive and she relied on Joe to get Holly ready in the morning before she crawled home feeling wearier than she could ever remember.

She was also trying to fit in visits to see Lucy, but it was sometimes difficult. At least when she was working at the hospital there was some advantage. It meant she could pop in to see her aunt during the rare, quiet periods. Lucy asked less and less about how they were coping at home, as her tests were clearly quite painful and she was left feeling sore and very weary.

'I can't possibly fit in this acupuncture session you've booked,' she told Joe the morning before she was due to go.

'Nonsense,' he insisted. 'I'll call in to see Lucy when I do my hospital visit this morning. She won't miss you for once.'

*   *   *

Anna gave in and later in the day, drove herself to the clinic with some trepidation. She had little idea of what to expect and was inhibited by the thought of some procedure she didn't understand.

'Mrs Kington. Anna, if I may call you that? Please come and sit down. I'd like to get a few details from you before we start treatment.' Bill Fletcher was gently spoken, a few years her senior. He exuded an air of confidence and she relaxed as she sat down.

'I understand from Joe that you've been undergoing severe stress for some time?' She nodded. 'And you're a midwife? I've done a lot of work for pregnant women and helped with childbirth too. But we're here to talk about you today.'

He took details of her situation and asked about medication, any physical problems she might have and she answered simply, feeling rather like one of her own patients. He took her blood pressure and felt her pulse, in several places. She eyed him curiously.

'I'm looking for the deep pulses. Signs of other things going on inside.'

'Do I need to close my eyes?'

'Only if it helps you to relax.'

'I'd rather watch what you're doing.'

He smiled, a gentle smile that made her feel confident.

He unwrapped tiny silver needles from sterile packs and began tapping them into various parts of her body.

'It is such an ancient medicine that we have to believe it works without fully understanding. Indeed, it has been proved to work for many people.' She lay still, totally relaxed and listening to his words. After about twenty minutes, he began to remove the needles.

'Now sit up slowly. You will probably feel a little light headed and very thirsty. I'd like you to sit in the waiting room for a few minutes and please, have a drink of water.'

Anna felt almost dreamlike as she floated through to the waiting room. She was more relaxed than she could remember for months.

'I have some leaflets you can take,' Bill told her. 'I'd be pleased to have the chance to work with you.'

'Thank you so much. I feel wonderful.'

Work that night was great. She had a couple of mothers brought in and looked after them without any problem.

One was still waiting by morning but the other had given birth to a daughter during the small hours. Though only a relatively short time, she felt refreshed.

'Maybe there's something in this acupuncture,' she muttered.

*　　*　　*

By the end of the week, Joe suggested that their system wasn't working. They had seen little of each other during the hectic working hours and when one was in, the other was out.

'I'm not sure we can continue like this,' Joe said on Saturday morning. 'I've got a day off and you are about to go to bed.'

'No. I'll stay up to be with Holly. I'm fine. Really.'

'No you're not. You're exhausted and you look terrible.'

'Thanks a bunch,' she replied in danger of bursting into tears.

'So, I have another plan. A much better plan.'

'We all give up work and go on a cruise for the next ten years?'

'That's one idea. But I thought you hated water?'

'I forgot.'

'Why don't we all move out to stay with Evie and Tom?'

'Don't be ridiculous. How could we?'

'They've got masses of space. Loads of spare rooms. Evie can look after Holly during the day and you can go back to normal working. Holly will enjoy being with the Terrors and I'm sure she'll be fine with them. Whatever I say about them being rough little tykes, they're very good hearted.'

'But what on earth does Evie think about all this? Assuming you've spoken to her.'

'Actually, it was her idea. I phoned to tell her where I was and why. She immediately suggested it. She seems to like you for some reason.'

'I'm really not sure. It's a long drive every day. Over an hour.'

'Not really, if you take a few shortcuts, you can do it in much less. I think it's an excellent plan. We can move over there today and get settled before Monday. You can't go on working these stupid hours. Two nights a week on call is one thing, but every night followed by days looking after a toddler, well, how long can you go on before you become ill as well as Lucy? You have a responsibility to your patients.'

She burst into tears. He put his arms round her and held her close. He gently stroked her back and she nestled closer, enjoying the comfort he was offering.

'Me want hug as well,' piped Holly as she came into the room, breaking the moment.

'Come on then, pipsqueak.' Joe hauled her up to their level and the three of them hugged together, every bit a family. 'Better now?' he asked. Anna nodded. 'Ready to move out to the country?'

'I guess so. If you're sure Evie and Tom won't mind.' She hoped he couldn't hear the pounding of her heart, which seemed to be filling her own ears.

'They'll be delighted.'

'We're going on a little holiday, Poppet. You'll enjoy staying with Sam and Jake, won't you?'

THE PAST RETURNS FOR ANNA

Anna was immediately made to feel at home. Evie and Tom were delighted to have them staying and she knew she would become great friends with Joe's pretty sister. She had the same greenish eyes and blonder hair than Joe's, but there was a great similarity. Her sense of humour was slightly less zany but still there.

Holly was entranced at having two surrogate brothers and followed them round like a puppy. They seemed happy to have her with them and played beautifully with the little girl. Anna enjoyed her time with the family and felt very much at ease with everyone, not least Joe.

Evie cornered her one afternoon. 'Is there something between you two or not?' she asked outright. 'I thought, that is, we thought that you were well, close.'

'Thank you but . . . I . . . I'm not really sure. There's certainly something between us but nothing's decided yet, if that's what you're asking.'

'I'm sorry if I'm being pushy, but I think Joe's in love with you. I hope you love him too, because I don't want him hurt.' Her face looked very serious, even a hint of a threat was in her eyes.

'Oh Evie, I'd never hurt him. But I'm not

sure how much of a future we have. I'm very scared of being hurt again. The loss of my husband, well it was almost too much to bear. If it hadn't been for Holly and Lucy, of course, I don't think I'd have survived. How could I dare risk it again?'

'But Joe's as reliable as any man could be.'

'I'm sure he is. But we haven't known each other all that long. And there's another problem for me. He risks his life on the lifeboats. How can I live with someone who goes out to sea in all kinds of weather? After what happened to Ben, I mean.'

'It's different. You couldn't ask him to give that up. It's something all our family do. The men at least. Even Tom goes out when needed.'

'But how can you live with that? Suppose he didn't come back?'

'I'm proud of what he does. What they all do. So many people owe their lives to our two men. I live with it because I have to. It's what they do.'

'I see. I'm still not sure I'm brave enough. I don't think I could bear another hero who thinks he's invincible.'

Evie looked slightly irritated but she said nothing. After a while she spoke again.

'Look, I'm happy to have you staying here and I love having another woman to talk to. I want us to be good friends. But I should warn you, if you ever do anything that hurts my brother in any way, I shall never forgive you. Nor will I forget it.'

'Evie, I promise you, if things do ever look like becoming more than I can manage, I shall be quite open about it and you can throw us out right away.'

'Come here, silly,' she said and pulled Anna into a hug. 'I realise you have problems and I'm sure everything will work out in the end. Maybe I'm being too impatient for my brother to settle down and be happy.'

'You know, I can't remember having a really close female friend for years. Thank you so much for your generosity.'

*   *   *

The days fell into their own routine and life was as happy as it could be, considering the worries over Lucy's health. She was not responding as everyone hoped and Anna was most concerned. She had read up about pernicious anaemia and knew that her aunt should have been feeling better by now, responding to treatment. She was discussing it with Joe one evening after supper.

'I know pernicious anaemia occurs when someone can't absorb folic acid. Vitamin B12. But I still don't understand why it produces these symptoms. Or why it suddenly becomes a problem. I mean to say, she's in her fifties and never shown any symptoms before.'

'There's a special chemical produced in the stomach. If there is insufficient produced, folic acid isn't absorbed.'

'Goodness. Thank heavens we got there in time.'

The phone rang.

'It's for you, Joe,' Evie called. He picked up the extension in the sitting room and Anna could hear his side of the conversation.

'I see. How far out are they? . . . So the big boat's needed? Right. And how many are injured? OK. I'll make sure I've got as much as I can carry. OK. See you in . . . well, as soon as I can get there. Bye.'

'What's that about?' Anna asked, already fearing the answer.

'It's a shout. I have to go. Medical emergency on a fishing boat off the north coast. Can't stop now. But I'm badly needed.' He rushed off and collected his medical bag on the way. She followed him into the hall and watched as he flung a waterproof jacket over his shoulders. He kissed her cheek as he rushed past, calling goodbye to everyone. Evie came to see him off and wished him luck.

'I don't really understand why they can't send a helicopter out to the fishing boat. It would be so much quicker. Why does Joe have to go out on the boat?'

'I gather the boat's too close to the cliffs for the helicopter to pick up the injured men. Tom's had the shout too. He's already left.

They have to take the big lifeboat out and obviously they need a doctor. The inshore boat would be too small if the men need taking off. They'll probably have to take the entire crew off and if the injuries are really severe, the helicopter will airlift them off the boat when it's further out.'

'How do you know all this? So quickly I mean?'

'It's a familiar story. Small fishing boat gets stuck on rocks and crew needs rescuing.'

'When will we hear anything?'

'Probably not for hours yet. If they've called for Joe, he'll have to treat injuries and that is always a long job in bad conditions. We should go to bed. There's nothing we can do to help and well, you have work tomorrow.'

'I'll never sleep,' Anna told her friend. 'I couldn't, not knowing they're out there.'

They made cocoa and sat in the warm kitchen clutching their mugs between their fingers for comfort. Anna asked how Evie could cope so calmly with Tom's life in danger.

'You don't think of the danger and simply pray that they are able to do their job properly. And come back safely of course.'

*   *   *

The situation for Joe was as bad as it could be. They had launched the lifeboat and bounced over the waves towards the site of the endangered fishing boat. It was caught on rocks only a few yards from the towering cliffs, so typical of the north coast. It was too close to them for the rescue helicopter and the lifeboat helmsman needed utmost skill and care to avoid being dashed on the rocks themselves.

There were four crew on the fishing boat, two of whom had suffered serious crush injuries when a winch had broken. Somehow, they had shot a line over from the lifeboat and organised a sling. Joe had been hauled across first to assess the situation. The boat was badly damaged and there was little hope of saving it. His main objective was to get the injured men to safety on the lifeboat and then the rest of the crew would attempt to rescue the others. He should be able to do something for the injured men.

'Can you tell me how these men were injured?' he asked.

'Wire cable snapped and let down the crate on top of their legs. We managed to get it off eventually but, well see for yourself.'

Joe staggered along the swaying deck, clutching at the rails and medical equipment as he made his way to the two injured men lying on the deck. They seemed to be in agony and he administered morphine to each of them to help with the pain. He used the radio to get the lifeboat crew to send stretchers over.

One of the men came with them and together, they managed to strap the first man securely on to the special rigid stretcher and carefully winched him across. The small boat groaned and shook as the waves battered her. Joe was afraid that it might break up at any moment but gritted his teeth and set about strapping on the second man. He had passed out with pain which actually helped them move him more quickly. It was better to risk further damage than lose him entirely. They got him across too and were beginning to feel more optimistic. The radio bleeped.

'You'd better get over here, Doc. This guy isn't looking too good.'

'But there are two more men over here,' he protested. 'They should come first.'

'You next, Doc. We need you here.'

'OK,' Joe agreed and apologised to the two shivering crewmen who were left.

'That's all right. Send the sling back as soon as you get there. This poor old lady's had it. We just need to get ourselves off her now.'

Joe was soon back on the lifeboat and began to treat his patients as best as he could. Their only chance was to get further out from the cliffs so the helicopter could get in and lift them off. They needed hospital treatment as soon as possible or both would lose their legs. The heaving boat prevented any proper treatment, even if he'd had the equipment to do it.

One of the men arrived from the stricken boat and the sling went back across. There was a huge crash and the lifeboat jolted violently. The sling and cables suddenly snapped and sank into the sea and they watched in horror as the man who was half way across fell down into the sea. The rescuers hauled on the wire, dragging the man towards the safety of the lifeboat. The fishing boat disappeared under the waves, leaving only a few pieces of floating debris as evidence it had ever existed. It was too close to the rocks and high cliffs.

They had shone powerful lights into the water, watching as the last man was hauled up the side of the boat. He was barely able to cling on but strong arms reached down and pulled him to safety. He was half drowned and they had to pump his chest to remove the water. Gasping for air, he coughed and spluttered and at least they all knew he was alive. The captain suddenly called out, 'We need to get clear.' The engine accelerated and they quickly left the dreadful scene. They organised a rendezvous with the air ambulance a couple of miles out and the injured men were lifted off. Both had broken legs and other injuries. Joe and Tom knew they had succeeded in their mission, though there were still worries about the fishermen. It took another two hours for them to get back to port and finally clear the boat.

'We did what we could,' the Captain told them. 'Thanks very much everyone. Get yourselves home now.'

Joe leaned back against the side of the boat and closed his eyes. He hoped that Anna had gone to bed. He could imagine what she was thinking and knew that this call possibly could be a crucial event in their relationship. How often had she said that she couldn't bear to live with another sailor? Silently, he mouthed the words. *Darling, Anna. Please love me. I'd do anything for you . . . even give up this work if it matters so much to you. Love me, Anna, I beg you.*

*   *   *

After lying awake till well after midnight, Anna went down to the kitchen to make another drink. She paced up and down, wondering how the rescue was going.

She could hear the wind howling round the old farmhouse and knew it would be much worse closer to the sea. The waves would be crashing against the rocks and sending spray high into the air.

The poor crew of the fishing boat would be getting drenched with each wave and the rescue team would have to fight against wind, waves and there was probably a time urgency too. Depending on the injuries, speed was often vital in giving proper treatment.

She shivered, thinking about the boats bouncing over the waves. She thought of Ben and again relived the memory of how it must have been for him to sink under the waves, his lungs painfully filling with sea water until he lapsed into unconsciousness.

It could happen again. To Joe or Tom. She hugged her arms round herself as tears fell.

She felt helpless and angry for being so helpless. She paced back and forth, knowing she was making herself feel worse all the time.

'Anna? What are you doing? Couldn't you sleep? Hey, come on. No need to cry.' Once more, Evie put her arms round Anna and hugged her close. 'Come on. Dry your eyes. This doesn't help you or them, you know.'

'But . . .'

'But nothing. Now, we're going to have another drink and then you're going back to bed. You need to be awake for Holly in the morning. They'll be back when they're back. Driving yourself mad with worry won't make any difference to them.'

Anna sat down near the Aga. She was still shivering and her fingers shook as she took the mug of tea from Evie.

'Whatever you say, I can see you really do care for my brother, don't you?'

'I suppose I must. I never expected to feel this much emotion ever again.'

'I'm glad for you. He's a wonderful man and deserves some happiness in his life. I'm sure he loves you too, as I've already told you.'

'I don't know if I love him. It's almost too strong an emotion. But I am very fond of him.'

'Who are you trying to convince? You love him. It's quite obvious. You need to come to terms with it. Your husband died three years ago. It's time to move on without the guilt. Now, bed for you.'

*   *   *

It was four o'clock before the two men returned. As soon as she heard the door open, Anna rushed down to see if they were all right. She flung herself at Joe.

'Oh thank heavens you're back. Are you all right?'

'I guess. Hey, don't look so worried. It's all right.' He held her in his arms, his wet coat soaking through her thin dressing gown. He stroked her hair and comforted her.

'I'm sorry. But I was so scared. Did you . . . were you able to help the injured men?'

The two men exchanged glances. Their faces looked drawn.

'We managed to get the two worst injured men off the boat and away in the helicopter. I don't know how successful their treatment will be. The others are OK. Shocked, but surviving. But the fishing boat was very badly damaged. It began to keel over and took only seconds to go down. Our own crew got off in time.'

'But you saved two men.'

'It's a dangerous life,' Tom added. 'But as always, you were good, Joe. Most professional.

119

He's a good bloke, your doctor. Now, I'm starving. No sign of Evie yet? I need a large bacon sandwich and several gallons of hot tea.'

'I'll make it,' Anna said as calmly as she could, despite the intense trembling she still felt inside. The activity helped calm her and soon she was feeling better. The intensity of emotion had left her feeling drained and she kept looking at Joe as if seeing him for the first time. He was strong and capable. Dependable.

Suddenly, she knew for certain that she loved him. The realisation hit her. But she knew it must not be allowed to happen. She couldn't face a lifetime of evenings like this one. This roller coaster life was not for her or her little daughter.

'There you are, chaps. Bacon sandwiches and tea as ordered. I'll leave you to it. Some of us have to work tomorrow.'

'Unfortunately, so do the rest of us,' Tom replied. 'This looks good. Thanks, Anna.'

*   *   *

Joe was rather silent for the next couple of days. He called the hospital where the other fishermen had been taken and both were going to recover, once they'd got over two broken legs apiece.

When the weekend came, they were both off duty. Anna suggested that she should go back home and leave Tom and Evie in peace for a couple of days. She wanted to make sure everything was ready for Lucy's return, whenever that was to be.

They'd left home so hurriedly that she felt concerned that she needed to check on things. Joe insisted on accompanying her and gladly, she accepted, knowing she would feel rather lonely on her own, with just Holly for company.

'I'll need to do some shopping,' she said. 'The fridge is virtually empty.'

'We'll go together and I can help with this little monster,' he said, holding Holly high in the air. She shrieked with joy and wriggled to get down.

'There's no need. I can manage,' she replied.

But he insisted and she had to admit, shopping with Joe was much more fun than shopping alone. He waltzed Holly in time to the bland music all along the aisles in the trolley seat. She sang as they went, much to the amusement of the other shoppers. Luckily the place wasn't crowded for once. He kept putting treats for them into the trolley, including packs of smoked salmon and a bottle of sparkling wine. He added fresh croissants and expensive apricot preserve.

They took Holly to the park for the afternoon and played on swings and fed bits of bread to the ducks near the pond. Anna felt relaxed and had to admit that she had thoroughly enjoyed what seemed like a family day out.

'We could go to the beach tomorrow, if you like,' Joe suggested later.

'Butick and spade,' Holly sang. 'Play on beach. Please Mummy. Wiv Joe.'

'Looks like it's decided,' Anna agreed.

Once Holly was in bed, they sat for a long time over their meal. They'd prepared a simple meal together and felt companionable and very comfortable.

'I've had a lovely day. Thank you, Joe.'

'I've enjoyed it too. Nice and relaxing. There's just one thing I need to make it perfect' He put his arms round her and drew her close. He kissed her. This time it was never Ben she thought of. It was one hundred percent Joe, kissing her. Comparisons were forgotten.

'Tell me you love me. I know you do but I need to hear you say it,' Joe demanded.

'I can't,' she sobbed. 'I daren't say it. I'm too afraid of losing you.' She closed her eyes as the tears pricked them. She had a vision of Ben's face . . . a face she had almost forgotten unless she looked at his picture. He had a slightly mocking smile, one she had seen so many times, but had never before realised was one which mocked.

'You haven't said you don't love me. Just daren't. That's probably hopeful,' Joe said with a smile. 'I think you love me, possibly approaching as much as I love you. As I once said to you, I usually get what I want, eventually. And, Mrs Anna Kington, I want to marry you, however long it takes. It's not just now but forever. You'll realise it eventually.'

'Maybe,' she murmured, staring up at his beautiful eyes and loving each part of his handsome face. Then she closed her eyes as a vision of Ben started to push his way into her mind.

'It's him, isn't it? He's haunting you. We'll get rid of him one day, I promise.'

'I'm not sure. I guess I never found closure. If the boat had been found, I may have been able to believe it.'

'I'm sorry if I can't live up to his high standards.'

'Joe. You must never think that. It isn't anything wrong with you. You're wonderful. But, I suppose you're right. I am haunted. How can I love someone else when I've been so unhappy for so long? With all that sorrow in my soul, I feel guilty at even considering loving anyone else.'

'We need to do something about it. Try to relax now.' She needed to move on. He had a plan in mind but he could not tell anyone what it was. Not yet.

He should never have told her he loved her. He'd scared her off and if his plan didn't work, he had probably lost the chance of happiness for ever.

'I'VE GOT SOME NEWS FOR YOU.'

'Gosh, I slept well,' Anna announced at breakfast the next morning. 'I certainly felt more relaxed than I have in ages. Must have been the food. And the company of course.'

'All part of the service. Literally,' Joe added. 'And for better or worse, I meant every word I said.' He looked very serious and she felt concerned that she couldn't ever live up to his hopes. But his mood lightened. 'Now, I've built up one huge appetite. Are we going to have the full works for breakfast?'

They cooked a huge breakfast and Holly sat chewing a sausage, held in her fingers.

Joe grinned. He wanted this woman and child in his life and he meant to make it happen one way or another. For him, this was true and hopefully, lasting love. If his plan worked, it would be the same for her. Eventually.

They spent a pleasant morning on the beach and went into the hospital after lunch as planned. Lucy was looking much better and was out of bed, sitting in a chair.

'They've finally sorted me out,' she said happily. 'They say I can come home on Tuesday. I'm not sure how we'll manage, but I promise, I won't need much looking after.'

'We've got it all arranged,' Anna fibbed.

'I'm taking a few days off and then I'm going on nights. Holly always sleeps through and once she's in bed, you can just be on hand in case she wakes. I'll be back home in time to take her to nursery and then I can catch up on sleep. See? All arranged.'

'Well, if you say so, dear. I must confess though, I can't wait to get back to my own home.'

Joe took Anna and Holly back home and asked if they still planned to return to Evie and Tom's house for the night.

'I think we'd better stay here now we know Lucy's coming back.'

'I need to go and collect my stuff and I guess I'll return to my lonely bedsit.'

'You could stay on here if you wanted to. I'm sure Lucy will be delighted.'

'Thanks, but it's best if I stay in my own place for now.'

'As you like.' Anna felt disappointed but she could see it was for the best. Somehow, she felt she had never reached such a closeness with Ben even after several years of marriage. With Joe, there was an instant understanding, a knowledge of what would please and never any sense of things being hidden from each other.

He was such a caring person and they seemed to understand each other's moods and needs without even speaking aloud. She suddenly realised that with Ben, there had often been the feeling that something was missing. That there was something he wasn't saying. She felt shocked at the realisation that their marriage may not after all, have been as perfect as she thought. Perhaps one day, this might enable her to get over her guilt.

'Explain to Evie for me will you? And say I hope to see them all again very soon. Can you collect any bits and pieces we've left there?'

'Of course. It also gives me the excuse to call round here, doesn't it?'

Anna arranged with the nursery to keep Holly for the whole of the next day. She needed to work extra hard to get her arrangements sorted for the coming weeks. She spent the morning visiting her regular patients and explaining to all of them that one of her colleagues would be looking after them for a few weeks. She might see some of them at the hospital, she told them, especially if they delivered during the night shifts. She drove out to see Sandy Pierce, anxious to know if she was still managing to keep her baby.

'I'm so fed up,' she announced. 'I'm staying in bed most days and getting up when Jack comes home. I'm bored silly.'

'You'll know it was all worth while when the little one finally arrives,' she encouraged. 'Let's see, where are you now?'

'Nearly thirty weeks. The baby might be all right if it's born soon, mightn't it?'

'We hope you'll hang on for quite a bit longer yet.'

'I hope I do see you for the birth. I feel as if we've become friends.'

'I'll do my best. You'll be in hospital anyhow, so who knows? How did you get on with the acupuncture? I'd like to have been with you, but work didn't let me.'

'It was great. I don't remember feeling so relaxed. He did say he'd come to the hospital when I started going into labour. I don't really understand it but it's something to do with median lines in the body. They have to be in harmony or equilibrium. It sounds a bit strange to me, but it seems that if everything is balanced the energy can flow properly. Whether it was this or my stay in hospital, I'm not sure. But I am still here and holding on.'

'The important thing is that you got something out of it.'

'What do you think about him coming to the hospital when I start?'

'I'll have to ask them. I wouldn't have any objections but then, I may not be the one to deliver you.' She completed her tests and was pleased to note everything was looking as good as possible.

She raced back to the Medical Centre in time for the weekly meeting. Everyone was sympathetic to her problems and murmurs of help were offered. They all said they would miss her in the Centre, but looked forward to her return when things were back to normal. Joe was remarkably quiet and said almost nothing to her after the meeting. But, as she was extremely busy, she didn't have time to brood.

The ante-natal clinic ended with the usual collection of questions and light banter. Finally she was free to collect Holly and return home. Holly was fractious and very tired after her day at nursery. Clearly, the long day was too much for the child and mornings only would have to be the routine. Could she survive on three hours sleep? For a while maybe, but there had to be some other way until Lucy was fully recovered. Briefly, she considered Ben's mother's offer to have Holly to stay and immediately discounted it.

'Come on, Holly. We have to go and do some shopping.'

'No,' she cried out, stamping her foot.

'Please be a good girl. Auntie Lucy's coming home tomorrow and we want some nice things to feed her.'

'Want Joe. Not you.'

Anna felt like weeping. She was tired and overwrought and really didn't want a confrontation with Holly. She might just manage the shopping on the morning, before she went to collect Lucy.

'All right. We'll leave the shopping for now. I'll get your tea and then you can have a nice bath and go to bed.'

'Want shopping wiv Joe,' she said firmly.

'Joe isn't here. It's me or nothing.'

'Nuffing. Nuffing,' she chanted. Anna cursed herself. She'd always known it was a bad idea to get close to anyone and this was exactly what she'd wanted to avoid. Her little girl had become fond of someone and missed him when he'd gone. She considered phoning him and asking him to supper but she knew it was a bad idea and gave herself lots of jobs to do. She finally fell into bed, exhausted. She knew she could be happy with Joe, but it wasn't fair to him if she constantly felt this awful guilt. Would it ever go away?

*   *   *

The next morning, she delivered a slightly unwilling Holly to the nursery and dashed to the supermarket before going to collect Lucy from hospital. At her aunt's request, she took in a large tin of chocolates for the staff who'd been looking after her.

'You don't have to worry about me, dear,' Lucy said as they got home. 'I'm feeling so much better. A bit sore where they've pumped all the various things into me but a day or two and I'll be back to normal.'

'You're not going to do anything for a few days. Just relax and be waited on for once. I'm on holiday till Friday and then I'm starting nights at the hospital. I've done a swap with one of the midwives there and she's taking over my rounds. Everyone's been very good about it. That way, I can look after you and Holly and get some sleep when she's at nursery. It's going to be nice to spend some time together.'

Despite her protestations that she was fine, Lucy was clearly still needing extra rest. She had definitely been diagnosed with pernicious anaemia and would need to be given medication for the rest of her life.

'You know, dear, I hadn't realised how bad my memory had been getting. I haven't been able to do my crosswords for months. But I can see now, it was all part of the symptoms. If your Joe hadn't spotted it, I might have got worse and worse. Where is he by the way? Isn't he staying here any more?'

'He's working, of course. And no, he isn't staying. He needed to get back to his own place.'

'Well, I hope you're going to invite him round one evening, soon. I want to thank him properly.' Wisely, she said no more, though she was curious to know how things were really progressing between them. She had high hopes for this particular relationship.

'Of course. I'll call him. Tomorrow, maybe? If you're up to it. I don't want you getting tired.'

Anna dialled the Medical Centre when she thought Joe would have finished his morning surgery. Maggie informed her that Doctor Meredith was taking a few days holiday.

'You mean he isn't staying with you?' Maggie asked surprised.

'Of course not.'

'Oh dear. We'd all decided you were about to elope and do us out of a party. Both being off at the same time, I mean.'

'I'd no idea he was taking a holiday,' Anna replied, feeling rather put out. Still, she had no right to think she would be told about everything he did. 'Thanks, Maggie. I'll be in touch.' She put the phone down and frowned. Then she dialled Evie's number.

'Hi, Evie. Is Joe there by any chance?'

'Joe? No. Haven't seen or heard anything of him since Sunday. How's your aunt?'

'She seems OK. I'm going to have a job to make her rest, but I'm working on it. I just wanted to say thanks to you again for everything. You were wonderful and I'm very grateful. Hope to see you soon.' They chatted for a while but clearly Joe's disappearance was a mystery to her too.

Lucy began to improve in many ways. She seemed more cheerful than before, though in all honesty, Anna hadn't even realised that her aunt had been feeling depressed. Nor had she realised that she had been finding difficulty in moving around for some months.

'Oh, Lucy, I feel so ashamed. I've been taking you for granted for far too long. How could I have been so blind?'

'Perhaps I'm a better actress than I thought.

Don't beat yourself up about it. All's well now. You have to get your own life sorted out. Time you began to live properly again. Time you forgot about that husband of yours and thought about the future for you and Holly. She needs a daddy in her life.'

'I suppose you'd prescribe Joe, would you?'

'You could do far worse. He's a good man and he is obviously fond of you and Holly. In fact, I'd half hoped you'd have some news for me when I came home? Spending time together, as you did.'

'We're very good friends. But I'm not ready for more. Not yet.'

*   *   *

The next few days were a quiet routine of building Lucy's strength and organising Holly. She kept asking for Joe but he seemed to have disappeared completely. Anna began to realise she had probably scared him off. Her response to him must have proved that she was a hopeless case and now he'd gone away. It wasn't only Holly who missed him.

Her first night on duty at the hospital was reasonably quiet. There were the usual ward rounds and new-born babies who needed night feeds, to organise. She even managed a bit of sleep in the staff rest room and was ready to start her day with Holly when she returned home. The one problem with the weekend was

132

that there was no nursery, so any sleep had to be snatched at odd moments when Holly was resting. Lucy listened for the child and promised to wake her when she was needed.

The next night was busier, with a fairly straightforward birth. There was no rest possible this time and she went home feeling totally drained. She tried to be lively for Holly but it was very difficult not to drop off to sleep whenever she stopped. Reading a book was fatal and Holly kept prodding her to get on with the story.

By the time her next duty started, she felt quite dizzy and she hoped desperately that there were no complications. It reminded her of student days when they worked all day, partied all evening and studied into what was left of the night. How on earth had they ever coped? The joys of youth, she assumed.

She walked along the hospital corridors to get herself something to eat before the canteen closed. She half wondered if she might meet Joe, as she had done once before.

'Where are you, Joe?' she whispered. She had come to rely on him and was missing him dreadfully. This was the painful part of loving someone. Made even more painful because she daren't tell him just how much she loved him. Even more than Ben? She wondered.

She shivered. It was too disloyal to the father of their child. How could she allow herself to love anyone more than Ben? He had been everything to her. He hadn't been able to help getting into financial difficulties. She just wished he'd confided in her before it had all gone so wrong. Poor Ben.

Not for the first time, she once more wondered if he'd killed himself deliberately. Scuppered the boat because he couldn't cope any longer. But as always, she pushed the thought away.

Not Ben. Never. He enjoyed life too much to ever end it deliberately. Fun loving, madcap Ben would never have ended it that way.

*   *   *

Anna had agreed to work five nights on and three nights off. It was a long time reaching the fifth night but in the long term, it should enable her to establish some sort of sleep pattern. She felt totally exhausted and longed for a proper night's sleep. Inevitably, when the time came, she found it almost impossible and thoughts of Joe and Ben whirled around her mind. Lucy was getting very worried about her and suggested that she must return to her normal routine right away and that somehow, she would cope. But Anna would not ever consider this and insisted that she was fine.

She finally got a call from Joe.

'I've got some news for you. I need to see you as soon as possible.'

'What is it? Where've you been all this

time? Nobody would tell me where you'd gone. I thought you'd left because you were sick of us.'

'Oh, my love. Of course not. Not directly, that is. When can we meet?'

'Tell me, Joe. Is it something terrible?'

'When can we meet,' he repeated.

'Now, if you like. I can't stand the suspense.'

'I want you to be alone. Can you arrange that?'

'Of course. Pick me up here and we'll go out somewhere.' Anna stood clutching the phone. Holly was in bed and Lucy was watching some television programme.

On pins, Anna waited for Joe to arrive. She had forgotten to ask where he was so had no idea how long he would be. She was in her old jeans and a scruffy T-shirt but changing didn't occur to her. He clearly had something serious to discuss and she was very scared of what it might be.

A SHOCKING DISCOVERY

Anna watched through the window for his car. When he stopped in the drive, she ran to the door. Joe put his arms round her and kissed her gently. He held her close and comfortingly.

'What is it, Joe? You're scaring me.'

'You'd better sit down. I have some news. News about Ben.'

Her face went pale and she felt the room suddenly seem to be swirling round. 'You've found his boat?'

'Yes. But there's more. Much more. I've been trying to think of easy ways to tell you this, but there is only one way. He isn't dead at all. I don't really know how to tell you . . . but he's alive and well. He's living in Santander. In Spain. I'm sorry. I mean, I'm sorry to be the one to tell you.'

Anna thought she was about to faint, but Joe put his arm round her for support and comfort. He was feeling almost desperate to know her thoughts but dared not ask. He wanted to take away the hurt. To love her better. To blot away all her pain. All he could do was to hold her.

Anna was conscious of every beat of her heart and the blood pounded round her head. She felt as if her feet were floating above the ground. She managed to whisper.

'But how could he be? How could he be alive and not get in contact with me? Let me think he was dead all this time? How could anyone be so unbelievably cruel?'

'Because he wanted it that way. It was a deliberate plan. He's changed his name and that of the boat. He planned it all carefully. I'm afraid there's something else.'

'What could be any worse?'

'He's got another partner. They went away together to start a new life.'

'So he must have cleared our bank account deliberately. And the second mortgage was to raise even more funds? And all this to make a new start with someone else. How could he? Surely he must have realised what this would do to me? To his parents? I find it impossible to believe. Not my beautiful Ben. He would never do this to me.'

Sobs wracked through her body as the whole truth was dawning. Three long years of grieving and all the time he was enjoying life with another woman. All the struggles she had to pay off debts. Joe put a hand on her shoulder but she shook it off.

He went to make some tea. He felt helpless. He'd known his plan might backfire on him. That it could lead to something like this and for the hundredth time, he asked himself if it had been the right thing to do. He'd thought about some of the things Anna had said when telling the story. He remembered the thoughts the lifeboat crews had at the time and the comments they'd made.

He'd had the feeling that Ben's disappearance had been too thorough and he had decided to go and search for him. It had been only a faint chance but he knew that Anna would always hold back with him, unless she finally found closure. If he had failed to find Ben then he would have gradually convinced her that he'd been lost. But he had been too successful and his worst nightmare had proved to be true. He took the tea into the sitting room.

'Come on, drink this. I know it doesn't help much but sipping it might stop you crying for a few minutes.'

'I need to know everything,' Anna told him. 'Right from the beginning. How, why . . . everything.'

'You once asked if it was possible that he meant to disappear and start again. It played on my mind. I know the sea is a large place but if he really had sailed where he'd said he was going, there would surely have been something found from the boat. So, I decided to follow it up. I checked a couple of marinas along the coast and found someone who remembered him. Ben was well known around these parts.

'This chap said he'd loaded up with stores and there'd been a woman with him. He'd thought no more about it and assumed as we all did, that he'd been lost at sea. I worked out

138

where he was likely to have gone and tried a few ports in Brittany to start with. Eventually, I went to Santander in Spain and bingo. There he was. He's running some sort of hire business, pretty much as he did here.'

'Utter swine!' she exclaimed. 'How could he? How could he hurt people so much? How did you recognise him?' Tears were streaming unchecked as she spoke through her sobs.

'You have photographs around the place. I've usually felt he was also haunting me a bit. Keeping watch to see I behaved myself. Then I mentally added a beard. That's the usual disguise. I was right.'

'What did he say to you?'

'You don't want to know. Words to the effect of you're welcome to her. Only ruder.'

'Did . . . did you tell him about Holly?' she whispered.

'I'm afraid so. I let it out when I was telling him what I thought of him. Apart from what he's done to you, I was pretty angry about the amount of time and money that was wasted by all of us looking for him. He'd sailed away in entirely the opposite direction, so even if he'd been spotted by the helicopter somewhere south, he may not have been recognised. He'd already painted over the boat's name and registration number. I really find it hard to believe he'd do this to you.' Joe rubbed his chin as if remembering something.

They talked long into the night. Questions

poured from Anna and always Joe tried to answer honestly and without prejudice. Evidently Ben had been shocked to learn about Holly and even seemed to show slight remorse at this point. Joe's greatest fear was that he might show up again to see the child or worse. He was much too afraid to ask Anna how she would feel.

'I think I should leave now,' Joe said at last. 'I'm due back at work in the morning. Shall we meet up at lunch time?'

'I'm not working at the centre at the moment. I've swapped with Joanna. I'm doing nights at the hospital. Just till Lucy's fully recovered.'

'I hope that will be very soon. The place won't be the same without you there.'

*　　　*　　　*

Lucy was understandably devastated when she heard the news and immediately tried to take charge again. They spent a lazy day, doing their best to shield Holly from the frenzy of feelings they both shared. Over and over she asked how he could have done it to her and his own family, but there was never an answer. Anna decided that it must have been life with her that had been so awful. Ben must really have hated her. Her confidence sank once more to rock bottom.

She went to work with a heavy heart. Her

hopes of possibly making a new life with Joe were completely dashed. Whatever Ben had done, they were still married. How could she ever marry anyone else? She could have been happy with Joe and without a doubt, Holly would have loved him almost as much as she did. Now she had to face seeing the handsome doctor every day at work, once she went back to the Medical Centre. It was almost too much.

He was probably going to stay on indefinitely, unless this turn of events made him change his mind. Her brooding was ended rather abruptly when a call came in to say the ambulance was bringing in a patient. It was Sandy Pierce. Her labour had started and though the baby was very early, they were all praying it would survive. Anna paged the consultant. He would need to be present for this one. She could not make any decisions on her own.

'Oh Anna, thank heavens for a friendly face,' Sandy gasped. 'I couldn't hold on any longer.'

'Bring her through here,' she told the ambulance crew. 'The doctor is on his way down.'

Anna pulled over the sophisticated monitoring devices and attached the pads to Sandy's tummy. She clipped the pulse peg to her finger and attached the blood pressure monitor. She watched the readings before examining her further.

'How long might it be, do you think?' asked Sandy anxiously.

'We'll know better when the doctor's seen you.' Sandy was sweating profusely and she got a face cloth and wiped her forehead. 'Where's Jack?'

'Sorry,' Doctor Grey said, as he came rushing in. 'What have we got?'

'This is Sandy Pierce. Thirty weeks. She's started labour. Not very far yet but you need to look at the foetal heart rate. Bit erratic. Down to sixty at times.'

The doctor made a thorough examination and listened to the heart.

'I was hoping we might be able to slow you down. Even stop the contractions, but I think we're a bit too late for that. We need to deliver this baby as fast as we can. We really need to do a caesarian section. Are you all right with that?'

'Oh, but I so wanted to have a normal birth. With Jack there too.'

'He can attend the birth, unless there are any problems. It may not be what you wanted but it's for the best. I'm afraid we might lose your baby, unless we hurry.'

'I'll let theatre know we're on the way. It really is for the best,' Anna assured her and once she'd phoned the theatre, began to prepare Sandy for the surgery. She'd spoken to the doctor and established the procedure to be used.

'We'll give you an injection which numbs all the nerves in your spine. You shouldn't feel a thing. I'll be with you all the time.'

'Thanks, Anna. I'm so glad you are here. It will be all right, won't it?'

'We'll do everything we possibly can. Look, here's Jack. I'll leave you to explain what's happening.' Anna hoped that giving her something to do would lessen her patient's anxiety. She went through to the small operating theatre to prepare herself and make sure everything was ready. For a baby delivered before term, they more often went to the large hospital at Truro, but there was no time.

The on-call anaesthetist arrived and everything was ready. Sandy was wheeled in and an anxious Jack followed, gowned and ready to play his supportive role.

The expert staff was soon delivering the baby and Anna immediately took charge of him, taking him to the table where a radiant heater shone down, making sure he was warm.

He was very tiny and having difficulty in starting to breathe. The staff watched as Anna worked on him, shielding him with her back to make sure the new parents were unaware of their anxiety. She cleared the mucous and gently coaxed his heartbeat. She gently flicked his feet to stimulate a reaction and rubbed him with a towel. She applied the oxygen mask to help him. Nothing.

She rubbed him again, doing everything she could to stimulate the fragile life. More oxygen until at long last, he gave a splutter. A thin wail came from him and everyone breathed a sigh of relief. She smiled and quickly wrapped him in a soft cloth and took him to his parents.

'Meet your son,' she whispered, her own emotions running high, as always. After the initial struggle, she felt even more moved this time. 'I'm afraid I need to put him in the humidicrib right away. He needs to be kept warm and we will need to monitor him all the time. You'll be able to see him soon.'

'I can't believe how quickly it was all over,' Jack was saying to his wife. He was still feeling stunned by his experience of being rushed into theatre so swiftly.

'I get the feeling it's all only just starting,' Sandy said feebly.

It wasn't long before she was back in a bed, sitting up and sipping tea.

'Your little boy's resting now. He seems to be holding his own,' Anna said.

'And you think he's going to be all right?'

'We hope so. Now, you need to rest. You can stay for a while Jack, but I recommend you go home and try to sleep. You'll need your strength once the family get home.'

'Family. That sounds good. After all this time, I thought it was always going to be just the two of us. Well done, darling,' he murmured to his wife.

Anna left them alone. How much she would have loved the closeness of a loving husband when she had given birth. Instead, he'd been sailing around the Spanish coast with another woman, leaving her believing she was a grief stricken widow, coping alone. She felt the surge of anger rising once more and wished she could talk to Joe again.

Dear Joe. He seemed so dependable and to think he'd done all that for her. For them, perhaps. Maybe if he'd known the outcome, he wouldn't have made such an effort. Perhaps she would have got over her guilt in time but now, she resented the fact that she wasn't free. However free Ben thought he was, she knew she was still married.

Joe had mentioned a divorce, but that still depended on Ben actually admitting his deception to the authorities. She still couldn't believe he could have got away with it for so long.

What on earth would his parents say? She gave a jolt. Ben's parents. They would have to be told. Mrs Kington was not in the best of health. The shock could be too much for her. And who was going to break the news to them? Not her, if she could help it. The bleeping of a monitor brought her back to her work and she swept into action.

Anna drifted along for several days. Joe called to them several times but she felt honour bound to keep him at a distance. He wasn't very pleased about it, she knew.

'I'd hoped to make things better, not worse,' he said ruefully. 'I begin to wish I hadn't bothered.'

*　　　*　　　*

After two more weeks, Lucy begged Anna to return to her normal working hours.

'I can easily look after Holly again, especially if we continue with the nursery school in a morning,' she assured her. 'And you look exhausted. I want to see some colour in your cheeks again.'

'We've really missed you,' Maggie told her when she returned to work during the day. 'And so has the gorgeous Doctor Meredith. He's been so serious nearly all the time since he got back from his holiday. Barely a joke in sight. Let's hope you get him back to his old cheerful ways.'

'I don't think I'll have much influence, actually.'

'Don't tell me you two have had a tiff?'

'Too complicated to discuss here. Have you got my list?'

*　　　*　　　*

When Joe came in, he went straight to her room and sat on her desk.

146

'How are you? Glad to be back?'

'I guess so. But nothing's really changed, for us I mean. I still feel as if I'm married to Ben, however awful he was. Is. What do you think he'll do? His parents have to be told.'

'Not your job. It's up to him now. I'm sure he'd have to give you a divorce.'

'I've got a patient coming in. I'm sorry, Joe. However much I wanted you, everything's changed now. It's over between us. It has to be. For Holly's sake as well.'

'I won't give up, you know. Never.' He left her staring after him.

'I do love you, Joe,' she whispered as tears were forcing their way from her eyes. She blinked them away and went to call in her patient.

When she returned home that evening, she failed to notice there was a car parked in the lane near the house. She played outside with Holly for a while and the little dog from next door came to join them in the garden. They threw balls for him and he bounded round, yapping with excitement. Holly made little yapping noises too and they all laughed.

'Man,' Holly called, pointing at the fence. Anna saw a movement and a trickle of fear went through her. She bravely crossed the garden and looked over. She saw a red car drive away but it was too quick for her to get the number. She felt unnerved and they went back inside.

'I don't know who it could have been,' Anna told her aunt. 'But I felt uncomfortable. As if I were being spied on.'

'Perhaps it was just someone walking their dog. The track goes down to the woods.'

'Maybe. But you should keep your doors locked when I'm not here.'

When she came home the next evening, she saw a red car parked in the lane again and went to see if there was a driver.

'Hello, Anna,' a voice said from behind her, as she peered inside the empty car. A shiver ran down her spine. She swung round, frightened out of her wits. She stared at the familiar figure with a face she almost didn't recognise.

'Ben?' she whispered. 'Ben?' It was like seeing a ghost. How many times had she longed for this moment, an impossible moment, or so she had believed for three years. Now, here he was standing in front of her. 'Ben?' she said again, disbelievingly.

'You're looking well, Anna.'

'You awful, awful man! Have you any idea what you've done to me? The absolute agonies you have put me through?'

'It wasn't ever meant to hurt you.'

'How can you possibly think that? You put me into huge debt. You took everything. And allowed me to grieve, thinking you were dead.'

'I didn't leave you with nothing. Not at all. You had my daughter. My beautiful little blonde daughter. I gave you something very precious.'

'She's my daughter. Mine alone. Nothing to do with you.'

'You're wrong you know. I've come back for you. For you both.'

'Well you can clear off again. After what you did to me? To us? I'm going nowhere with you and you're not having Holly. Not having anything to do with her.' Her heart was pounding and her knees seemed to have turned to jelly but she managed to stay her ground.

'Oh, but you're wrong. Any court will allow me access. I can claim that I've been suffering from amnesia. After all my traumas, getting lost at sea. Head injury during a storm. Got blown off course. Poor Ben. Couldn't even remember his own name. But I can now, and I'm here. Ready to take up where we left off.'

'Nobody will believe that. You were seen with your other woman, loading the boat for a trip. I'll tell the police.'

'Says who? You're coming back with me. We're going to start again, as a proper family.'

'Rubbish. You can go back to your . . . to your other woman. Who ever she is.'

'There is no other woman, darling. There was only ever you.'

'Not what I heard.'

'She's gone. Didn't know I was a family man. She upped and offed.'

'But Joe said . . . '

'Oh yes. It was all thanks to the not so charming doctor friend of yours. She had never suspected a thing till he turned up. Doctor, eh? So you weren't playing the grieving widow after all.'

'How dare you. Just leave or I'll call the police.' Her voice shook with anger. Her emotions were running riot.

'Why not? Call them. Call the police. I can tell them my story and how my ungrateful wife has been getting cosy with one of the local GPs while I was suffering from amnesia. Look good for your precious practice won't it?'

'I'm not worried about the practice. It's Holly and me that I have to consider.'

'Just think how much she'd enjoy living on a boat. And the Spanish climate is wonderful. All that sunshine.'

'No, Ben. Never. I couldn't ever go through that again when you found something else to grab your attention. You've simply no idea how much I suffered. You've ruined the past three years of my life. I'm never risking that again.'

'HE'S STILL MY HUSBAND.'

'Anna? Where are you?' Lucy called. 'Only we saw the car and were waiting for you to come in.'

'I'm just coming,' she shouted. 'And you're just going,' she snapped at Ben.

'I'll call round later to meet my daughter and the most worthy Aunt Lucy. She'll be pleased to see me, I'm sure.' He got into the car and drove off.

Trembling, Anna went inside. She put the chain across the door and went to check the back was locked.

'What is it?' Lucy demanded. 'What's wrong? And why are you locking the doors?"

'Ben. Ben's here. He was waiting outside for me. He wants to see Holly. He wants to take her away from me. Well, he says he wants both of us to go with him.' There was a note of hysteria in her voice. She was still shaking.

'I thought he might.'

'But he can't. I won't let him,' she almost screamed.

'I think he should see her. You can't really stop him and we don't want an unpleasant court saga, do we? I think he should be allowed to see her, but only under our strict supervision. That way he won't turn even nastier.'

'I can't believe this. I can't believe it after all he's done. How can you support him?'

'I'm not supporting him. Not at all. I'm sorry to say it, but he is still your husband.'

'He says he'll be back later. Do you really think I should let him see Holly?'

Lucy nodded. She went into the kitchen and brought Anna a mug of sweet tea. Holly followed her, clutching her beloved Mister Teddy.

'Bin sleeping, Mummy.' She came over for a hug and Anna lifted her on to her knee, holding her close. She was so precious. Nobody would ever harm a hair on her head, not as long as she had breath in her body. Lucy put the tea beside her. When the doorbell rang, she nearly knocked it over.

'I'll go,' insisted Lucy. Anna held on tightly to her daughter and sat tensely, trying to hear who was there. To her relief it was Joe.

'Hello, you two. My favourite ladies.' Holly climbed down from her mother and rushed to Joe to be lifted high in the air. She cuddled into his arms and put her thumb in her mouth, totally content. 'Is there something wrong?' He looked at Anna's white face, her blue eyes looking huge, tear filled as they were.

'Shall we get some tea for Joe, Holly? Come and help me.' Joe raised his eyebrows.

'Ben's turned up. Wants to see Holly and claims there is nobody else. No other woman. He wants us to go to Spain with him,' she told him, her words tumbling out desperately.

'Don't be ridiculous. He must be crazy to think you'd have anything to do with him. You wouldn't? Would you?'

'He said he'd drag you into it and sully the good name of the practice. I don't think Doctor Whittaker would be too pleased if there was any scandal.'

'Hey now, hang on. What have we done that could cause any sort of scandal? Everyone knows you thought that Ben was dead. Besides, nothing has ever happened between us.' His eyes were filled with concern and Anna longed to fall into his wonderfully comforting arms. But everything had changed now.

'He is still my husband and he is Holly's father.'

'He gave up any rights to that when he sailed off. With another companion, don't forget. Whatever he says, I definitely saw a woman with him.'

'He says she went off when she discovered about the child. That it was your entire fault. He says he's coming to see Holly later.'

'Would you like me to stay around?' How she longed to say yes but she knew it would provoke her . . . her husband. She forced herself to acknowledge the word.

'I think that would only make matters worse.'

'Oh hell, what have I done? I only took this

course of action because I wanted to make sure you were free of him. I never dreamt all this might happen. I thought the chances of really finding him were so unlikely as to be ridiculous but it was a chance I needed to take. Now I've made matters a whole lot worse.'

Anna stood and went to him. He pulled her into his arms and held her tightly. His heart was racing, as he held the most precious woman he'd ever known. The woman he now feared he was in danger of losing. 'Anna, oh Anna,' he whispered into her hair. 'I love you, Anna, with all my heart. I want you to be mine. Please be very careful what you do. And I beg you, come back to me safe and sound.'

'Oh, Joe. I do love you, you know I do. But this whole situation prevents us from being together. I'm not sure I can go through with a divorce. For Holly's sake.'

'But you can't stay with that man. After all he's done to you? He's unstable and he might even try to snatch Holly. He'd still leave you grieving, only this time it would be much worse. You'd be without your daughter.'

With tear-filled eyes, she held on to this man, to whom she had at last admitted her love. Her voice shook as she spoke.

'Every child has the right to know its father. And whatever sort of man he is, he is still her father. And I did love him once. Very much. He wasn't always like this. He's changed.'

Joe sighed and turned away from her. He

drew in his breath to speak again but thought better of it and turned away. His actions had turned everyone's world upside down.

'Joe,' she whispered, but he had gone.

*   *   *

Trying to behave as normally as possible for Holly's sake, she and Lucy had some tea and at last it was the child's bedtime. Anna took her upstairs to bath her, wondering if they were to escape the threatened visit this evening. She jumped at every sound but managed to read a story to the little girl without interruption.

'Mister Teddy, Mister Teddy,' Holly chanted.

Anna went to fetch the bear and saw a figure standing outside the door. The bell rang. Her heart pounding once more, she opened the door and let her husband into the house.

'I hope I'm in time to see my daughter,' he said.

'She's in bed. I'd rather you didn't confuse her before she goes to sleep.'

'Very well. Perhaps Lucy can find me a bed for the night and then I can see her tomorrow morning. I'm planning to be a big part of her life.'

'Stay here? I don't think so. I'm just going to take her teddy to her and then we'll talk. I'll tell Lucy you're here. Please be careful not to

155

upset her. She's been unwell.' She went into the kitchen to update her aunt on developments and took the teddy upstairs.

Ben was still standing on his own in the hall when she returned. She led him into the sitting room. He was like a familiar stranger. She offered him a drink and he took it wordlessly. She poured one for herself, feeling in need of something to stabilise her racing emotions. It was more than a little strange to be standing in the same room as him after all this time. All the anguish of the past years. A weird, waking dream.

How many times had she seen someone in a street and thought it was him? Only to feel bereaved all over again when it turned out to be someone else. And now, here he was standing right there in front of her as he had in so many dreams over the past three years.

'You're looking good, Anna,' he said.

'You too,' she replied honestly, in a voice that shook. He was as handsome as she remembered him. It was with a shock that she recognised how little he had changed from the man she had once loved so much. The whole situation was almost too bizarre. She felt she was in some sort of dream.

'I know sorry is meaningless. I think I was overtaken with some sort of madness. Flattered by the attention of a glamorous, younger woman. And I was terrified by the thought of losing everything. The business was collapsing and I didn't dare tell anyone. Least of all you. But, enough of all the drama. I hope it isn't too late for us. It's a great life out there in Spain. Sun and sea. Holly would love it. You'd love it. Will you at least think about it?'

She was incredulous. How could he even ask? 'My life's here, Ben. I have a job I love. I couldn't leave Lucy now. After all I went through. The debts and everything. You left me with nothing. You'd cleared the bank. You'd taken out a second mortgage. Can you imagine the shock I had when I realised how much the monthly payments would be? And you'd even let the life policy lapse so I didn't even have that to help me. As your body wasn't found, we couldn't do anything for months.

'All the time I was being sick with the stress as well as the pregnancy. I was grieving for the husband I adored. I was forced to sell our lovely home. Then there was an inquest looming, which was even more hell to go through. I think you have the most colossal nerve even to think I might consider staying with you.'

'I didn't realise it was all so traumatic. I didn't know anything about our baby. I thought you'd manage everything, as you always do . . . I'm sorry.'

'Oh, you're sorry. That makes it all fine then, doesn't it? Your parents think it was all my fault anyway. I should have noticed you were unwell. I should have called the coastguards sooner. I shouldn't have sold the house. You name it. They clearly hate me for what they think I failed to do for you.

'How could you put them through it all? They adored you and your mother has been unwell ever since. Your father claims she has some sort of heart condition, brought on by your absence from their lives. But, despite everything, I suppose you are Holly's father and you have a right to see her, but only under supervision. You may not take her out of this house nor be alone with her at any time.'

'I suppose Lucy put you up to that.'

'If you must know, it was Lucy who made me realise you do have a right to see Holly. Personally, I would never have let you anywhere near her.'

'I assume you want a divorce? So you can be with your doctor?'

'No. Whatever I feel about you, I can't go through a divorce. I know that Joe and I can't be together now.'

Ben smirked at her words. She realised that she didn't even like him any more. He wasn't the idolised man she had thought he was. The idol had feet of clay. He was unfeeling insensitive and he had a nasty, mocking look in his eyes. How had he conned her all those years? She'd always considered herself a good judge of character. But she wasn't. Not in Ben's case. Unfortunately, he was still her

158

husband and also Holly's father, she reminded herself.

*   *   *

They talked for several hours. Lucy came in and spoke briefly but it was clear she didn't want to spend any time with him. Despite her better judgement, she had agreed he could stay in the spare room for just one night, if he really had nowhere else to go. He promised he would leave soon after breakfast, once he had met his daughter. If he slept at all, Anna had no idea.

She lay awake most of the night, thinking of what might have been and pondering over what was to be. She tried to remember the good times with Ben but always, his recent actions and what she had discovered about him, overrode everything and she knew she would never trust him again. Her heart was drawn to Joe, the man she knew she loved but could no longer have.

*   *   *

The meeting between Holly and her father was horrendous. Something she wanted to forget. Her daughter had thrown a huge tantrum and refused to speak to Ben. He'd tried to say he was her daddy but she pointed at the photograph insisting that was her daddy. She did not recognise his face from the picture, presumably because he had a beard. He offered to shave it off but Anna refused.

'Want Joe. Want Joe,' Holly yelled and threw her bowl of cereal over the floor.

'It seems to me that this little lady needs some strong discipline,' Ben announced. 'She clearly has been spoiled.'

'Don't you dare criticise,' Anna said coldly. 'It's your fault she's behaving like this. What do you expect, arriving unannounced and demanding to take over? You could never expect Holly to accept you. Love and respect needs to be earned. Lucy, will you be all right? I'll drop her off at nursery and then I must get to work.'

Lucy agreed meekly that she was fine. 'I want you to leave, Ben. Right away please.' He held his hands up in mock surrender and left the room. It was some time later that she heard the front door slam and breathed a sigh of relief 'I'll collect Holly at lunchtime and bring her back here. You will keep the door locked, won't you?' He may have left for now, but she knew she hadn't yet seen the last of him.

Joe was waiting anxiously when she arrived at work, slightly late. She told him what had happened and he looked even more worried.

'You actually let him stay under the same roof as you and Holly? Are you completely mad?' She reassured him that all was well and

160

that he had now left. 'He won't give up so easily. He's mentally unbalanced. He has to be. Turning up and expecting everything to return to the way it had been before. Please be very careful.'

She tried hard to concentrate on her work, but it was very difficult. She visited some of her new mums and for brief moments, was able to share their pleasure. Sandy and Jack had returned home and their little boy was being discharged later in the week. They were excited but nervous of their new responsibility. Anna reassured them and said she would be calling in each day once the baby was home.

All too soon it was time to collect Holly and she knew the effects of a sleepless night were taking their toll. She stayed at home for some lunch and rushed back to catch up the ante-natal class. She had just arrived back at the Centre when her mobile rang. It was Lucy.

'Sorry to bother you, dear, but did you take the back door key with you? I meant to ask when you were home but I forgot.'

'No. I haven't got it. Oh dear. Do you think Ben could have taken it?'

'Crumbs, I hope not. Perhaps Holly hid it somewhere. She was in a funny mood this morning. Don't worry. I'll find it.' Anna closed her eyes. Her life had become a nightmare in a few short days. How was it going to end?

ANNA FACES DANGER

There was no sign of the key and when she mentioned her concerns to Joe, he insisted they should get the lock changed. There was no way Ben should be allowed access to the house. He was clearly unbalanced and might even try to snatch Holly. That was enough and she immediately phoned a locksmith. It was a difficult few days, even though they heard nothing more from Ben.

'Anna dear, have you seen that box of teaspoons?' Lucy asked when she arrived back. 'The little silver ones? I can't think where I put them. I thought I'd polish the silver this afternoon and they were missing. I'm worried I put them somewhere silly, when I was ill. I'm beginning to discover just how many stupid things I was doing over the past weeks.'

'Aren't they in the sideboard? I'm sure I saw them there recently.'

'I've mislaid so many other things too.' Lucy looked both ashamed and agitated.

'Such as?' Anna asked worriedly.

'Oh my rings. Other bits of jewellery. I can't think where I might have hidden them. And there's my emergency money. You know your uncle and I always kept a little store of cash for emergencies. In case we needed something and couldn't get to the bank.'

'I didn't realise you still kept it. Was there much?'

'Well yes. I think there may have been about two thousand pounds.'

'Two thousand pounds!' she gasped. 'You can't be serious. Why on earth did you have that much money in the house?'

'Well, we got into the habit of drawing out a few pounds each week. I just carried on doing it and well, I suppose I just never seemed to use it. It mounted up over the months.'

'Oh, Lucy. Why didn't you tell me? You should never have kept money in the house. I definitely think that we must have been robbed. Maybe Ben took the things. He must have come back into the house before we realised the key was missing.'

'Oh, surely not. He would never steal from us. I can't believe it of him.'

'I don't know what to believe any more. He's certainly no longer the man I married. I begin to think he's capable of anything. Well, at least he can't get in any more, not now the lock's been changed. But when could he have done it?'

The phone rang.

'Anna? It's Joe. I hate to ask you at this time, but I need some help. It's Evie. I don't know if you realised but she's pregnant again. Only there's something badly wrong. I'm going over there now but Tom's away on business and someone has to look after the kids. I hoped you might see what you can do for her and I'll stay with the kids. I wouldn't ask but well, it's all a bit desperate.'

'Joe . . . I don't know what to say. We've got a . . . a situation here too.'

'Please, Anna. We need you. Bring Holly with you. She can stay with me overnight if necessary.'

'Why don't you phone the hospital? There's bound to be someone on duty.'

'She won't let me. She wants you to be there. Says she trusts you. Much more than me. Besides, being family . . . well, you know.'

'I'll see what I can do.'

Eventually she was persuaded, and called Joe to say she was on the way. She waited outside the door until she heard Lucy fasten the lock and safety chain before she drove out to Evie and Tom's farm.

*   *   *

Evie was in a dreadful state when she arrived. She was grey with pain and lying on the sofa, refusing all attempts to get her to bed. Joe had got the boys to bed and was ready to assist in any way he could.

'Can you describe what's been happening?' Anna asked.

'I'm only about seven weeks on. Everything seemed fine and I'm booked for a scan next week.' She paused as pain surged through her

164

body.

'I'm afraid you may have an ectopic pregnancy. We have to get you into hospital as soon as we can. You'll need a blood transfusion and we must stop the bleeding quickly.' She glanced at Joe who nodded his agreement.

'Exactly what I thought. But even though he's a fully qualified, experienced doctor, a little brother can't be right.' Joe held his sister's hand as he spoke. Evie smiled wanly. 'I'll phone for an ambulance. It might take them a while to get here,' he warned as he dialled. 'Nobody can ever find this place.' He snapped out instructions to ambulance control and said he'd meet them at the bottom of the lane to make sure they didn't waste a second.

'What does it mean? Ectopic?' Evie asked anxiously.

'The baby is growing outside the womb. It tries to attach itself to something and well, there are lots of problems, Evie.'

'How can the baby survive?'

'Evie, my dear. It can't possibly survive. I'm so sorry.' Even amidst her pain, she wept for the loss of her baby.

'I know what's happened . . . with your husband,' Evie gasped. 'Joe told me what he'd done, trying to find him. He's grieving now. Grieving because he thinks he's lost you and it's all his fault.' Her words were stilted but she felt the need to speak. 'Please, Anna. He did it for the best. Don't leave him now. He wants you . . . loves you so much.'

'I know. I love him too, but Holly's father still has rights and we are still married, whatever he's done. Now, try not to upset yourself even more. Don't try and talk.'

'But . . . will I be able to have another baby?' she asked.

'You'll need some time to recover from this. But we'll have to wait and see what implications there are after this operation. There's no reason why you shouldn't after a while.

'Here they come. Would you like me to come with you? I can follow the ambulance and meet you at the hospital.'

'It's all right. But thank you. I'd much rather you stay here and talk to Joe. There must be something you can do. I want to see my little brother happy again.'

'I'll call in at the hospital tomorrow morning to see you. They'll operate right away so you'll be out of pain very soon and then you can sleep.'

The paramedics were soon carrying her out to the ambulance and Joe was making comforting noises, telling her not to worry about the boys or anything else.

'I did offer to go, but she said not to. She wanted me to stay and sort things out with you.'

'Marry me, Anna,' he asked suddenly. She

blinked tears away.

'I can't. I'd love to Joe, but you know what I said and nothing's changed.'

'Please don't tell me that . . . that man's going to win? After all he's done to you? You're an intelligent woman. Don't get sucked into his world again. He'll hurt you again, I'm telling you. At least give me some small hope.'

'Joe . . . I . . . there's nothing I can do. I can't make plans yet.' He grabbed her and kissed her. He held her so tightly that she could scarcely breathe. Tears coursed down her cheeks and she felt faint. He let her go.

'I'm sorry, my darling Anna. I shouldn't have done that. I'll be waiting for you. However long it takes.'

'I should go now. I do love you, Joe. But that's the only thing I can say. I don't know if it gives you any hope or not.'

She drove home, her eyes were blurred with tears. It was almost midnight and she was totally exhausted. She would have to wake Lucy to let her in, unless she'd released the safety chain before she'd gone to bed.

She tried her key and the door opened. The safety chain had been removed. Perhaps it wasn't a wise idea but at least it meant that she needn't disturb her aunt. Barely stopping to brush her teeth, she almost fell into bed and instantly fell asleep. She awoke refreshed and went for a shower before Holly arose. She dressed in her uniform and hair still damp, went down to put some coffee on. She turned as the kitchen door opened.

'Morning, Anna,' said a male voice. She dropped the coffee pot and screamed. 'Ben. What on earth are you doing here?'

'Just getting up. Like old times isn't it? You, me and a pot of coffee.'

'But you left. I told you I didn't want you here.'

'But your aunt made me feel so welcome, it would have been churlish not to stay on. Why were you so late? Out with the boyfriend?'

'Not that it's anything to do with you. Now, I'd be obliged if you were to get out of our house. How did you get in, anyhow?'

'Took a key conveniently left in the back door, but you changed the lock. Very silly of you. But it was all right. I took the spare front key too, just in case. And very conveniently, the safety chain was left undone.' Anna remembered the spare key which Joe had returned to the pot in the kitchen. He must have hunted round to find it before he left.

'And did you also take Lucy's things? Her jewellery? Cash and all the rest of the missing things?'

'Of course not. She's obviously put them somewhere safe. You must realise your aunt is in a bad way. Her mind's dodgy. She's not fit to be left in charge of my daughter. She should be put in a nursing home right away. It would mean you'd have this house for yourself. For us.'

'Get out. Now. Before I call the police. I'll give you ten minutes and then I phone them.' She was so angry at his words that she could scarcely speak. He ignored her and sat down and asked for coffee. 'No way,' she spluttered. 'You have five minutes left.'

Ben went upstairs and she could hear doors opening and closing. She heard Holly's voice and ran into the hallway. He was coming down the stairs carrying the protesting child.

'We're going for a nice day out, aren't we darling?' Ben was saying. 'She's my daughter and I'm going to take her with me. We'll have lots of fun. Call the police if you must but it will be a long time till you see her again.' Holly was screaming in terror.

'All right. I won't call them but you put her down. Right now.'

'Mummy, Mummy,' cried the little girl. 'Don't like man.' She held her arms out to her mother and Ben let her go. Anna grabbed her and held her close. Ben shrugged and went out of the door.

'Leave the keys you stole,' she called after him but he laughed and went off down the drive. Almost crying with relief, she went to find Lucy. She must have slept through everything.

'Oh Anna, is everything all right?' Lucy asked when she was finally woken up. 'I couldn't sleep and so I took a couple of pills. I

169

left the chain off the door for you. I didn't know when you'd be back and thought I might not hear you.'

'Oh Lucy, my dear. It's OK.' She told her the whole story of Ben's extra night spent under her roof and the threats he'd made. 'I know I should have called the police but I was so afraid he might take Holly. I'm sorry, but we have to change the locks yet again. All of them this time. And we'll get locks put on the windows too. I'm not taking any risks.

'I'm sorry but I really have to go to work now and I want to look in on Evie before I start. Will you be all right? I think you should keep Holly with you today. He might try to take her from nursery. And both of you, stay inside with everything firmly locked until the locksmith gets here.'

Anna found Joe already sitting by Evie's bed. He'd dropped the boys at their school and come straight here.

'I feel as if someone kicked me in the stomach,' Evie said weakly.

'I'm just so sorry for you. But it looks as though everything was caught in time. Before any more serious damage was done.'

'I should have insisted on calling the ambulance when I first got there,' Joe chided himself 'But I never could boss my big sister.'

'And have you two sorted out your problems?' Evie demanded.

'I'm afraid they seem insurmountable at the

moment,' Anna replied. 'I really don't know what's going to happen. But, you're not to worry. Try to get better soon, 'cos we all need you.' She leaned over and kissed Evie's cheek.

They walked out to the car park together.

'Any more news this morning?'

'You mean like Ben breaking in and sleeping in the spare room again? I didn't even know he was there until he walked into the kitchen. I nearly died of shock.'

Joe's face turned red as if he was about to explode. 'Don't, Joe,' Anna begged. 'It's all right. I've already booked a locksmith to change all the locks and fit new ones on the windows. It feels a bit like shutting the stable door but we need to do something.'

'You should contact the police. Get a restraining order on him.'

'He threatened me with taking Holly. Said he'd challenge for custody.'

'He doesn't stand a chance.'

'Maybe not. But even thinking about it fills me with horror. And he's stolen all manner of things. Well, we think he has. Lucy isn't convinced she hasn't put them somewhere silly. He took two thousand pounds and several pieces of jewellery, that we know of. Maybe there's other things too that we haven't noticed yet.'

'Then you really must report him to the police.'

'But he says he'll find a way to take Holly if

I do. I couldn't bear it Joe.'

She began to cry again and once more, he put his arms round her to comfort her. Her head rested against his shoulder. He drew in his breath, furious that this man should be able to threaten Anna and Holly. He had never felt such hatred for anyone before and vowed he simply must do something. Physical violence was against his nature but he really felt this time he might have to get satisfaction from crashing his fists into the man's face. He was boiling inside as he stroked Anna's soft hair.

'I'm sorry, but I have patients who'll be waiting for me. I didn't let them know I'd be late.'

It was a long morning and Anna felt disconnected from reality. By lunch time, she was feeling physically sick.

'Maggie, I'm sorry, but I'll have to go home. I really don't feel well. Can you ring my afternoon patients and let them know?'

'Don't worry about it. You do look dreadful,' Maggie told her. 'Maybe Lynn can come and take over for you. I'll give her a call and see if she can cover for a day or two. You need a break after the last few weeks. Is your aunt any better?'

'Lucy's fine, thanks. Just a few new family problems have come up.' She daren't tell Maggie the full story. It was all too complicated and she didn't feel capable of speaking about it without bursting into stressed tears.

She arrived home, much to her aunt's concern.

'What is it dear?' she asked.

'I'm just exhausted. I wanted to be home, here with you and Holly, making sure that we don't have more unwelcome visitors. Has the locksmith been yet?'

'This afternoon. Holly's having her nap at the moment. I'll get you some lunch. I don't expect you've eaten anything.'

'Oh Lucy, I'm so sorry to have brought all this trouble to you. You've been fantastic and now it seems never ending.'

'Nonsense, dear. I love having you here and once this business is sorted out, we'll soon be back to normal.'

Their conversation was interrupted by a scream from upstairs. They both rushed out, fearing the worst. Had Ben broken in again? Holly was lying on the floor beside her bed.

'What happened?' Anna asked.

'Mister Teddy felled out and I felled after him. Banged head.' Anna picked her up and cuddled her close. There was no real damage and she rubbed the little red patch. She looked into her eyes and the pupils were even so she felt sure there was no chance of concussion. But she would need to keep a close eye on her for the afternoon to make sure the child showed no symptoms or drowsiness. Just one more problem to add to the list, she thought.

ANOTHER TRAGEDY OCCURS

Anna was on tenterhooks for the next few days. She was constantly looking behind her and watched Holly keenly, every little thing she did. She was finally persuaded to allow the little girl to go to nursery to give her a break from the house and hopefully, to relieve the pressure they all felt. She had given strict instructions to the nursery supervisors that the child was never to leave unless she collected her. On no account was she to leave with any man who might come to take her, especially one claiming to be her father.

'No problem,' the kindly woman assured her. 'We have a very strict policy on the matter. Only the person we know who brings the child to us is allowed to take her away.'

Anna went into work and began her day. Almost as soon as she walked into the Medical Centre, there was a call for her. One of her patients, Emma, had started her labour and it was to be a home birth. She hoped for an easy delivery but asked who was the on-call doctor, just in case she might need help.

'It's Joe,' Maggie told her. She sighed. Why did it have to be him? She had been avoiding him all week, not daring to allow herself any time when they might be alone. It was all too difficult.

'OK. Well, you'd better make sure he knows where I am in case he's needed. Should be plain sailing but well, you never know.'

She drove out to the little house, near the edge of the village. Emma was in her room.

The labour was slow. It was going to be a long day. Anna phoned the Medical Centre to explain and asked if she might be relieved by her colleague later in the day. Maggie was apologetic and said that the other midwife had also been called out. The hospital was busy and someone was off sick there. There was no-one else who could take over.

She phoned home and Lucy assured that all was well. There was the slight problem of collecting Holly. After her request that nobody else should be allowed to collect her, she was in something of a quandary. After looking at her patient once more, she felt certain that it would be safe to leave her for the few minutes it would take to collect her daughter and deliver her home. The family seemed quite happy about it so she dashed off.

When she returned, only twenty-five minutes later, things seemed to have been speeding up.

'Anyone in,' called a voice from downstairs. Anna closed her eyes in gratitude. It was Joe.

'You're a miracle,' she called out. 'I was just about to phone you, or an ambulance.'

'I'm not going into hospital,' Emma said firmly.

'What's the problem?' Joe asked.

'Occipto-posterior presentation, I think.' Her voice was soft as she used the technical term to the doctor.

'Good Lord, whatever's that?' asked Emma.

'The baby's chin is pushed down on the chest and it can't flex the neck to negotiate the birth canal.'

'We'll see what we can do,' Joe said, taking off his jacket.

'I think we should call the ambulance just in case,' Joe said. Anna did so, explaining the situation and telling them to hurry.

'You're doing really, really well,' Anna told Emma a few minutes later.

At last the baby was born and Anna quickly took him knowing she needed to get the breathing going quickly after such a long wait.

'It's a lovely little boy,' she called out. He quickly took on a healthy pink look and the all-important cry came from him.

'The ambulance is here,' Anna said.

'It's too late.' Joe ran down to speak to the driver.

Joe apologised and explained the situation.

'The baby decided to come quicker than we thought. We were too busy to cancel the call.' They chatted for a few minutes and the ambulance drove away.

Anna cleared up and suggested Joe should leave.

'You must have finished your shift by now.

·Lucky you weren't called somewhere else.'

'Afternoon off,' he replied.

'And you stayed here all that time? Over and above the call of duty, Doctor Meredith.'

'Only way I get to see you these days. There's really nowhere I'd rather be.'

*   *   *

It was well into the evening before the doctor and midwife left the house and family to their new responsibilities.

'How's the Ben situation?'

'Quiet. Haven't heard from him again.'

'Do you think he's given up and gone back to wherever?'

They talked for a while, speculating, each of them tense and neither quite daring to say what they really wanted to.

'It was good working with you again.' Joe leaned in through the window as Anna sat in her car. 'Thanks for letting me stay and share.' She smiled as she drove away.

*   *   *

'Can we have a drink together this evening?' Joe asked after work the next day. Though she was dubious about leaving Lucy and Holly alone, she was persuaded. They needed to clear the air and talk through some of the problems that still surrounded them.

'I'll have to go. My car's being serviced and I have to collect it.'

'I'll give you a lift.'

'Well, if you're sure you don't mind. Thanks.' They had only driven a little way when he pulled over and stopped.

'I have to sign my new contract tomorrow,' Joe informed her. 'I only want to commit myself if we can find some less agonising way of working together. Otherwise, I'll pursue my usual drifting way of working and find somewhere else to go.'

'But I thought you'd already agreed to stay on.'

'I haven't signed anything yet. But, if you think there could be a future for us, well, I shall sign without a further thought.'

She was spared from answering when his pager bleeped.

'Blast. I should have told you that I was on call. There's a shout so I have to go. Can you get a taxi back?'

'I'll come with you now and then get a taxi if I need to.'

He didn't argue and they ran to the car and drove to the next village where the lifeboat was kept. She didn't like to admit that she'd thought it was a medical emergency rather than the lifeboat but it was too late. She expected to be left back at the Medical Centre. She sat in the car watching as the crew donned waterproof gear and the large boat slid down

178

the runway. Joe gave her a wave as they went. She waved back, shuddering at the thought of them going out to sea.

It wasn't a bad evening but someone needed them so they had to brave the weather, whatever the weather. She would wait for a while and then get a taxi if it looked like being a long trip. She watched till the lights were a distant blur. She went into the lifeboat station and spoke to the man in charge.

'Can you tell me anything about the shout? I was out with Joe and I wondered if you've any idea how long he's likely to be out there.'

'No idea, I'm afraid. You can come inside if you like. Have a coffee? I've just put the kettle on. You his missus then?' he asked in a rich Cornish accent.

'No. We work together. I'm wondering if I should get a taxi home. Where have they gone?'

'Got a call from a fishing vessel. Said they saw a yacht, looked as if it was drifting about five miles offshore. Tried to call them but couldn't raise them at all. Broken mast, they could see. Thought it might need investigating. It looks as if it might be one they've reported missing from down the Cradock Marina. Went missing a couple of days since. It's the right size and colour.'

Anna sat silently. Missing yacht? She knew someone who was prone to stealing stuff. Would he steal a boat? He was supposed to have his own boat in Spain, or so he'd told her. But this was ridiculous. Dozens of boats must be taken every year. Why should she think this one had anything to do with Ben? All the same, she couldn't help thinking this was a strong possibility.

'Do they have any idea who might have taken it?'

'All they've got is some closed circuit footage. You can only see a tall blondish bloke with a beard. Standard issue of anorak and jeans.'

'Would they let me see it? I think I might know who it is.'

'Is that right? I'll give the coastguards a call. They're looking for any leads. Expensive boat it is. Loaded with gear. There's a reward offered, I understand. But that wouldn't be why you're interested, I assume?'

'Of course not. But it's in my interest to know if it really was my husband who stole that boat.'

'Your husband? But I thought . . . Joe . . . never mind. I'll put that call through.'

They arranged for Anna to go and look at the security tape the next day. She waited in the lifeboat house, chatting to the officer. A little later, she heard the call come through from the lifeboat to say they'd reached the yacht but there was nobody on board.

The mast had broken and it was impossible to sail it home. It would have to be towed.

They were going to search the sea around it but there was no hope for whoever had been the crew of the yacht. She had a dreaded sense of déjà vu. She'd been through all of this once. She couldn't stand it again. At least this time, the boat had been found. Surely Ben, if Ben it had been, couldn't have faked his disappearance yet again? If he hadn't faked it, then it meant he was dead. Drowned. The irony didn't escape her.

Hours later, the lifeboat returned, towing the boat behind it.

'What are you doing, still waiting here?' Joe asked as he came wearily into the station.

'Waiting for you. I needed to know you were back safely.' He pulled her into his arms and hugged her before pressing her mouth against his own.

'All right, Doc. That's enough of that. Wait till you get her home,' called one of the crew good-humouredly.

Soon, Joe was driving her back. She told him of her suspicions, that it was Ben who'd stolen the boat and that this time; the missing man was indeed her husband.

'So all evening, you've been waiting to see if we brought Ben back, or his body.' She gave a shudder but agreed.

'I'm going to look at some security tapes tomorrow. I might be able to identify the man who was seen hanging around the marina.'

'And if you do identify him, we might find

fingerprints on the boat to match his. Have you got something with his prints on?'

'I daresay.'

'Excellent. We'll have him.'

'But Joe, we don't have him. You haven't found him . . . his . . . body. It's exactly like the last time.'

'I'm not sure I should tell you . . . but there's a lot of blood on the mast. We think it must have dropped on top of whoever was sailing the boat. He must have been badly injured or even killed. If it was Ben, there's no doubt about it. He couldn't have survived.'

She felt sick. She'd had to get used to Ben being dead for three long years. She'd had to accept that he had survived and was alive again. Now it seemed he really was dead, even though there was still no body. She was numb. The man had done everything bad that she could imagine but she was still married to him. He had terrified her with threats of taking Holly away, but he was still the child's father.

The car stopped outside her home.

'Will you be all right, Anna?'

'I have to be, don't I?'

'I'm so sorry. Much as I hated the thought of him, I wouldn't wish this on him. I'll pick you up in the morning and we'll go to see the coast guards together.'

'IT'S TIME TO MOVE ON.'

The owners of the boat identified it and were delighted to have it returned, even with the broken mast. Joe collected Anna and drove her to look at the security tapes from the marina. They watched it together, his hand firmly holding hers. They looked at the flickering television screen and Anna drew in her breath feeling tense, half hoping she wouldn't recognise the thief. As the shadowy figure walked along the gangway, she knew instantly that it was Ben. The rangy gait of his walk and the way he held his head were unmistakable. He glanced into the camera once and she could see the blond hair and beard.

'It's him,' she whispered. 'I'm absolutely certain of it.'

The police came to take fingerprints from the house as well as Joe's, Anna's and Lucy's, to eliminate them from any prints that Ben had left. Some time later, they learned there were numerous matching prints found on the stolen boat. They also took DNA samples from the mast, which they were able to match up with some hair left on the pillow when Ben had stayed.

'This time, I think your husband is truly dead,' Joe said gently. 'It's time to move on.

Time to begin your new life.'

'I hope you're right.'

'But you're going to tell me you still need to see his body before you'll properly believe it?'

'I'm sorry, but I think I might,' she whispered. Even now, she found it hard to believe that Ben was really dead. After three years of trying to come to terms and believing it, this second round of the same, was almost too much to cope with.

Joe spent some time looking at charts and tide tables. With any luck, a body would be washed up along the coast somewhere north of where they were. He was fighting hard against his instincts to take hold of her and love her. She would never know how tough it was to see her, to be close to her and have to force himself to turn away. If he hadn't loved her so much, he doubted he would have stayed in the practice any longer.

Life settled back into some sort of routine. Each day, he gave Anna something special to try and make her laugh. The first morning back at work, there was a little handbag mirror with a smiley face on it. Another day flowers were waiting on her desk. She opened her medical bag another time and found an idiotic little monkey. What a thoroughly kind man Joe was.

Joe was a regular visitor to the house, but he knew that he still needed to tread carefully with the woman he loved. But once this drama was over, they would have all the time in the world.

It took three weeks for Ben's body to be found. This time there was no doubt. Joe was able to spare Anna the trauma of identification, and he had been wearing a life jacket with the stolen boat's identification marks on it.

'Once the funeral is over, you'll be able to move on.' Lucy told her, hugging her closely. She felt saddened herself at the thought of losing her niece and the child she'd become so fond of. But she wanted Anna's happiness and knew that would be guaranteed with Joe Meredith.

'I'm dreading it. Meeting Ben's parents again under these new circumstances will be unimaginably horrible.'

'You'll have Joe and me beside you. We're going to support you every inch of the way.'

The difficulties she had experienced telling them about Ben's demise had proved almost too much. She had driven to visit them to break the news, bravely refusing Joe's offer ·to accompany her in case it inflamed the situation.

She almost tried to spare their feelings and keep his behaviour a secret but she knew that would be impossible. She even controlled herself when his mother had suggested it was her fault, that Anna had herself driven Ben away from them all.

'I shall organise the funeral and you are of course, welcome to attend. But I don't want to hear any more of your vile accusations or your insinuations about me.' She had left them standing silently. She still couldn't help feeling sorry for them. However horrid they had been, they had still lost their only son and they were frail and elderly.

When the dreaded day arrived, Anna was feeling calm and detached. Holly was spending the day with Evie and her family and had gone off very happily. It was a simple service with only a few friends and Ben's parents. When it was over, they went back to Lucy's house for a meal. Mr and Mrs Kington had said very little and accepted a plate of sandwiches and some tea.

Ben's mother looked pale and seemed to be detached from the proceedings. Her husband noticed that she was sweating and swayed slightly as if she was dizzy. She clutched herself as a spasm of pain throbbed through her body. She groaned loudly.

'Thelma, dear. Are you all right?'

Suddenly, her cup slipped from her grasp and she collapsed sideways in the armchair.

'It's all right. Stay back,' Joe commanded. He loosened the top button of her blouse and felt for her pulse. It was there but weak and thready. Anna rushed to fetch his medical bag which he'd left in the hall cupboard and handed him his stethoscope. He acknowledged her with a nod. Lucy ushered the other guests into the kitchen and began to make fresh tea. Mr Kington was pacing anxiously, wanting to get back to his wife.

'Leave it to Joe and Anna. They know what they're doing,' Lucy ordered him.

'But who is he? This Joe person? Does he really know what he's doing? Seems to be very much in with the family.'

'He's one of the doctors with Anna's practice.'

'I see. And was he the cause of Ben running away? Is he really Holly's father? She looks like him.'

'Mr Kington,' Lucy said angrily. 'Shut up. We've heard enough of your nonsense over the years. I don't know if you realise just how much you've hurt my niece but she's in there, with Joe, Doctor Meredith, trying to save your wife's life.'

'I'm sorry. I'm scared. I don't want to lose Thelma too.'

'I know. Now, have a cup of tea and try to sit down quietly for a while.'

In the sitting room, they'd got Thelma on the floor and were trying to keep her heart beating with massage.

'I've got some oxygen in the car, with the maternity kit.' She hadn't taken the cylinder back to the Medical Centre after her last home birth. She collected it and a fresh mask. 'I presume it's cardiac arrest, isn't it? They mentioned she may have a problem when I last went to stay. I should have taken it more seriously.'

'I've got a heartbeat. She's breathing again. Have you got any soluble aspirin? There should be some in my bag, if not.'

Anna found the little pills, so common yet so vital and handed them to him. He gave her one and fitted the oxygen mask over Thelma's nose and mouth.

'I'll get a blanket and then I'll phone for an ambulance.'

Everyone except Mr Kington had left by the time the ambulance came. He went with his wife to the hospital. Joe decided that Anna's need was the greater and elected to stay home with her.

'We make a good team,' he told her. 'Thanks for your help, though I did wonder for a moment whether you would feel able to.'

'What a day. What a way for it to end. I really do feel that I have now said goodbye to Ben and probably his family as well. They may think they want to keep in touch for Holly's sake but somehow, I doubt we'll hear much more of them once Thelma's out of hospital.'

'That's the first time you've ever used her name,' Joe remarked.

'Think it is. She never invited me to use it and I certainly could never have called her Mum. She always rather scared me. Somehow though, seeing her lying on the floor, so frail and ill, I realised she's just a sad old lady. Ben was her whole life and to have the facts uncovered about his true nature, well, it must have devastated her.'

'So now, we can move on? Truly?'

'Yes please,' she whispered.

'That sounds like a decision to me. And you, usually so slow to make decisions. I like this new Anna. Come here.' He swept her into his arms and kissed her.

'I expect you'll be wanting to find somewhere new to live,' Lucy said sadly as she watched them from the doorway.

'Lucy. We're going to be married,' Joe said letting Anna go and rushing to grab her aunt.

'Are we?'

'Course we are. Right away.'

'I'm delighted for you both.' Lucy sounded sincere but there was a huge lump in her throat. Her life was about to become lonely again, when they moved out. 'But I shall miss you all terribly.'

'Do you want us to find somewhere new to live?' Anna asked sadly. This was something she hadn't considered but she could hardly expect her aunt's generosity to extend any further.

'Well of course I don't. I can't bear the thought of living alone again, but you won't want a doddery old lady living with you.'

'Oh Lucy . . . if you'll let us stay here, we'd love it, wouldn't we darling?' Joe said.

'Of course we would. If you really wouldn't mind. Oh and you're not a doddery old lady by the way.'

'Oh, my dears, that's wonderful, quite wonderful.' They put their arms round each other.

Holly came in from the garden, covered in mud.

'I want hugs as well. And I want Joe for my daddy. Please.' They all stared at the little girl. How could she have understood all that was going on?

'Sam and Jake said Uncle Joe's like my daddy. Auntie Evie wants it too.' Her words sounded clear and firm, much more than her usual baby babble. She was growing up.

'Well, that's great. I am going to be your daddy and your mummy is going to be Mrs Meredith. Very soon.'

'A fambily,' she squeaked.

'Yes, darling, we're all going to live together and be a very happy family.'

'You know my dears, I've had a bottle of champagne ready for this day for simply ages. Thank heavens we can use it before it is quite past being drinkable.'

'To what I know will be a very happy family,' Lucy said, raising her glass a few minutes later.

'To happy families and to the midwife's new husband,' Anna said.

'And me,' squeaked Holly. 'To me as well.'

They all laughed and raised their glasses to

Holly. She smiled happily and lifted her cup of orange.

'Fambily,' she said happily.

.

15